AVID

READER

PRESS

THE
FARAWAY
WORLD

STORIES

PATRICIA
ENGEL

AVID READER PRESS

NEW YORK   LONDON   TORONTO   SYDNEY   NEW DELHI

AVID READER PRESS
An Imprint of Simon & Schuster, Inc.
1230 Avenue of the Americas
New York, NY 10020

First Avid Reader Press hardcover edition January 2023

AVID READER PRESS and colophon are trademarks of Simon & Schuster, Inc.

For information about special discounts for bulk purchases, please contact Simon & Schuster Special Sales at 1-866-506-1949 or business@simonandschuster.com.

The Simon & Schuster Speakers Bureau can bring authors to your live event. For more information or to book an event contact the Simon & Schuster Speakers Bureau at 1-866-248-3049 or visit our website at www.simonspeakers.com.

Interior design by Carly Loman

Manufactured in China

10 9 8 7 6 5 4 3 2 1

Library of Congress Cataloging-in-Publication Data has been applied for.

ISBN 978-1-9821-5952-8
ISBN 978-1-9821-5954-2 (ebook)

*For my mother and father
and for Matías*

We are what we
are what we never
think we are.

—SONIA SANCHEZ, "PERSONAL LETTER NO. 3"

And your otherness is perfect as my death.
Your otherness exhausts me,
like looking suddenly up from here
to impossible stars fading.
Everything is punished by your absence.

—LI-YOUNG LEE, "THE CITY IN WHICH I LOVE YOU"

CONTENTS

THE
FARAWAY
WORLD

AIDA

THE DETECTIVE WANTED TO KNOW IF AIDA WAS THE SORT OF GIRL who would run away from home. He'd asked to talk to me alone in the living room. My parents stood around the kitchen with the lady cop and the other detective, an old man who looked to be on his last days of the job.

I sat in the middle of the sofa, my thighs parting the cushions. The detective sat on the armchair our mother recently had reupholstered with a fleur-de-lis print because the cat had clawed through the previous paisley. The old-man detective was telling my parents Aida would walk through that front door any minute now. She probably just got distracted, wandered off with some friends. Our mother wasn't crying yet but she was close.

He looked young to be a detective. He wore jeans with a flannel shirt under a tweed blazer even though it was August. He wanted to know if Aida ever talked about leaving, like she had plans beyond this place, something else waiting for her somewhere.

I shook my head. I didn't tell him that since we were eleven, Aida and I kept a shoebox in the back of our closet under some long-forgotten stuffed animals that we called our Runaway Fund. The first year or two, we added every extra dollar we came across, and when our piles of bills became thick and messy, we took them to the bank and traded them for twenties. We planned to run away and join a group of travelers, sleep under bridges beside other refugee kids, and form orphan families like you see in movies and Friday night TV specials. Those were the days before we understood how much our parents needed us. Aida insisted on taking the cat with us. Andromeda was fat but could fit in her backpack. Aida had lied to our parents and said she found the cat alone one day by the river behind the soccer field, but she'd really bought her at the pet shop with some of our runaway savings. I didn't mind. The cat always loved her more than me though.

"Does she have a boyfriend? Somebody special?"

She didn't. Neither did I. Our parents told us boys were a big waste of time, and we kept busy with other things. School. Sports. Jobs. Painting classes for Aida and piano lessons for me. Our parents said just because we were girls who lived in a small town didn't mean we had to be *small-town girls*.

"Did she have any secrets?"

"Not from me."

"Even twins keep secrets from each other."

He made me tell him all over again what happened even though I'd gone through it several times in the kitchen while the old-man detective took notes and the lady cop leaned against the refrigerator, arms folded across her blockish breasts. The young detective said he'd keep whatever I told him in the strictest confidence. "If there's something you left out because your parents were around, now is the time to tell me, Salma."

"There's nothing," I said, and repeated all I'd already told them. How Aida was coming off her summer job as a gift wrapper at the children's department store at the bottom end of Elm Avenue while I was sweeping and cleaning the counters before closing at the coffee shop on the top end, where I worked the pastry case. We had this routine: whoever finished her shift first would call to say they were on their way to the other. Or we'd meet halfway at our designated third bench on the sidewalk in front of Memorial Park and we'd walk home together. That night, a little after seven, Aida had called and said, "Sal, I'll come to you." When she didn't show up, I took my purse and walked across the intersection to the park. I sat on our bench for a few minutes before walking the park periphery to see if maybe she'd run into some kids from school. Aida was friendly with everyone. Even the dropouts most everyone in town avoided though they hung around the bus station and liquor store, and you couldn't walk through the park without getting a whiff of their weed. Aida had a smile for everyone. People liked her. Sometimes I got the impression they just tolerated me because we were a package deal.

I called her phone but she didn't answer, then I tried our parents to see if they'd heard from her. It started from there. The calling around. Probably for the first time ever, the town employed that emergency phone chain, where each person is assigned five others to call, to see if anyone had seen Aida. Around here you can't get a haircut without it being blasted over the gossip wires, but nobody knew where she was. This is a town where nothing terrible ever happens. There are perverts and creeps like anywhere else but never an abduction or a murder. The worst violent crime this town ever saw beyond an occasional housewife wandering the supermarket with a broken nose or split lip was back in 1979, when one sophomore girl stabbed another with a pencil in the high school cafeteria.

The old-man detective reminded us we had the good fortune of living in one of the safest towns on the East Coast.

"This isn't some third world country," he told our mother. "The likelihood that your daughter was kidnapped is extremely remote."

He told our parents it was common for teenagers to test boundaries. If he only had a dollar for every time a parent called looking for a kid who it turned out had just taken off to a rock concert at the Meadowlands or hopped in a car with some friends and headed down the shore. And it'd been only four hours, he emphasized. Aida couldn't have gotten very far. Our mother argued that four hours could take her to Boston, to Washington, DC, so far into Pennsylvania that she might as well be in another country. Four hours was enough to disappear into nearby New York City, her dark pretty face bleeding into millions of others.

But the old detective insisted, "Four hours is nothing, ma'am. You'll see. You'll see."

•

Our mother and father arrived late to parenthood. Our mother was a spoiled Colombian diplomat's daughter who spent her childhood in Egypt, India, Japan, and Italy. She never went to university but was a dinner party scholar, a favorite guest, and indulged her international friendships for two decades of prolonged escapades in Buenos Aires, Los Angeles, London, Marrakech, and Barcelona. She had many boyfriends, was engaged three or four times but never married. She was a painter for a while, then a photographer, and an antiques dealer. She sometimes worked in boutiques or found a man to support her, though she never wanted to be tied down. She was thirty-eight when she met our father in a Heathrow airport bar. He was a shy history professor from Marseille who'd written three books on the Marranos of the sixteenth century. She thought he was boring and lonely yet stable, tender, and adulating; everything she needed at that particular moment in her life. They married and tried to have a baby immediately, but our mother had several disappointments until she received the good news of twin girls at the age of forty-four. We were born during our father's sabbatical year in Córdoba. Our mother said those prior broken seeds had been Aida and me but neither of us was ready for our debut.

"You were waiting for each other," she told us. "You insisted on being born together."

Our father never liked when she talked that way. He said she was going to make us think we had no identity outside our little pair. Our mother insisted this was the beautiful part of twinship. We were bound to each other. We were more than sisters. We could feel each other's pain and longing, and this meant we'd never be alone in our suffering. When Aida was sick, I'd become sick soon after. Our father blamed it on practical things like the fact that Aida and I shared a bedroom, a bathroom, and ate every meal together. Of course we'd pass our germs around, be each other's great infector. But our mother said it was because we were one body split in two. We'd once shared flesh and blood. Our hearts were once one meaty pulp. Our father would scold our mother for her mystical nonsense, and our mother would shoot back that he was always dismissing her; just because she didn't have fancy degrees like he did didn't make her an idiot. She'd cry and it would turn into the song of the night, with our mother locking herself into the bathroom and our father calling through the door, "Pilar, don't be like that. I just want them to know that if anything should ever happen, they can live without each other."

He wanted us to be individuals while our mother fought for our bond. We knew we held a privileged intimacy as twins, but Aida and I were never exclusive or reclusive. We had other friends and interests away from each other, yet it only made our attachment stronger, and we'd run into each other's arms at the end of each day, reporting every detail of our hours apart.

Ours was a brown Tudor house on a slight hill of a quiet block lined with oaks. Aida and I lived in what used to be the attic. It was a full-floor room with slanted ceilings and strange pockets of walls, so we each had niches for our beds, desks, bookshelves, and dressers, with a small beanbag area in the center. There was an empty guest room downstairs that either of us could have moved into, but we didn't want to be separated, even as Aida's heavy metal posters took over her half of the walls and she started to make fun of my babyish animal ones. We liked living up there even though it was hot in the summer and cold in the winter. We couldn't hear our parents' late-night fights once we turned on our stereo. Every now and then we'd lower the volume just to check in, see how far into it they were so we could gauge how long before we'd have to go downstairs to help them make up.

Aida and I considered ourselves their marriage counselors. It was like each of our parents had an only child; I was my father's daughter, and Aida belonged to our mother. When the fights became so bad we weren't sure they could make it back to each other on their own, Aida and I would assume our roles. I'd find our father alone in his study hunched over his desk or slumped in the leather reading chair staring out the window at nothing. Aida would go to their room, where our mother was always on the bed lying fetal in her nightgown. Aida would tell me that our mother would often ask her who she loved best, and Aida would declare her devotion to our mother and say that if our parents ever split, Aida and our mother would run off together to Paris or Hong Kong. Aida would always tell me this part laughing because we both knew she would never leave me and I would never leave our father. That was our trick. That's how we kept our family together.

•

Fliers of Aida's face went up on every telephone pole and shop window in town. Though the detectives briefly tried the idea that she'd run away, it was a missing person case. The police searched the town. The detectives made rounds of the homes of all Aida's friends. They focused on the boys, especially the ones with cars. But Aida wouldn't have gotten into a car with someone she didn't know. Our mother was mugged in Munich in the seventies and sexually assaulted behind a bar in Mallorca in the eighties. She raised us on terror stories of vulnerable wandering women being jumped by aggressive, predatory men. We were each other's bodyguards, but when alone, which was hardly ever, we were both cautious and sensible, even in this stale suburban oasis. If held at gunpoint, Aida would have run. She had long muscular legs, not at all knock-kneed like me, and the track coach was always trying to get her to join the team. Aida was a brave girl. Much braver than me. She would have screamed. She would have put up a fight. She would not have simply vanished.

A group of local volunteers quickly formed to comb the grass of Memorial Park, hunt for witnesses, go to every apartment and storefront with a view of the avenue and back alleys. The story made it into the evening news and morning papers and a tip line was set up for people to phone in. Our parents didn't leave the kitchen. Our mother waited, an eye on the front door, for Aida to show up in yesterday's clothes. Several people called and said they'd seen her the night before just as the summer sky began to blacken. She was in cutoff shorts, brown leather boots, and a white peasant blouse that had belonged to our mother. They'd seen her at the bottom of Elm, and someone else had seen her further up, approaching the park. She was alone. But someone else saw her talking to two young guys. Someone saw her later on. A girl in cutoff shorts and brown boots walking along the far side of the park across from the Protestant church. But she was in a blue shirt, not a white one. That girl, however, was me.

Aida and I hadn't dressed alike since we were little girls and our mother got her fix buying identical dresses to solicit the compliments of strangers. But the day Aida disappeared, we'd both put on our cutoffs, jeans we were now too tall for so we took scissors to them and made them shorts, though every time we wore them our mother warned we'd grown so much they were pushing obscene. We'd also both put on our brown gaucho boots, sent to us from one of our mother's friends from her bohemian days in Argentina. We were both running late for work that day, and that's why neither of us decided to go back upstairs to change.

One of the volunteers found Aida's purse by the Vietnam Veterans' monument in the middle of the park. Her wallet was inside, though emptied, along with her phone, the battery removed. Our mother wanted to take the bag home, but the police needed it for their investigation. The only other things they found were her lip gloss and a pack of cigarettes, which was strange because Aida didn't smoke. Chesterfields, our father's brand, probably swiped from the carton he kept on top of the fridge. The box was almost empty. I would have known if she'd been smoking, and our parents wouldn't have particularly minded. They were liberal about those sorts of things; the benefit of having older parents. They served us wine at dinner and spoke to us like colleagues most of the time, asking our opinions on books or art or world events. They'd trained us to be bored by kids our own age and to prefer their company over anyone else's. We had no idea how sheltered we really were.

•

In the days that followed, there were more sightings of Aida. Somebody saw her cashing a check at the bank. Somebody saw her cutting through the woods along the train tracks. Somebody saw her by the river behind the soccer field. Her long dark hair. Her tan bare legs in those same frayed shorts, though this time she was wearing sandals. And each time our parents would have to tell them it wasn't Aida they'd seen. It was her twin.

Three different people called to say they'd seen her, the girl whose photo they recognized from TV and the papers, hitchhiking on a service road off the turnpike near the New York State border. Someone else had seen her at a rest stop a few miles down. A woman had even said she'd talked to Aida at a gas station in Ringwood and only realized it was her after she caught the news later that night. She'd asked Aida where she was headed, and Aida had said north, to Buffalo.

Aida didn't know anybody in Buffalo, and she'd never take off. Not like that. She worried about everybody else too much. When we were little, she would say good night to every stuffed animal in our room before falling asleep, without skipping a single one so she wouldn't hurt anyone's feelings. She wouldn't leave the house without letting everyone know where she was going. I'd joke that she had separation anxiety and she'd say, "No, it's just love, you moron." Even so, after I heard the bit about Buffalo, I went up to our room and knelt on the closet floor until I found our old shoebox under the dusty pile of plush animals. It was empty, but I knew she couldn't have taken our money with her. Two years earlier we'd used the savings to buy our parents an anniversary gift of a sterling silver frame for their wedding picture. We'd depleted the funds but started adding money to the box again. Not much. Just dollars here and there whenever we had some to spare. We didn't think of it as our Runaway Fund anymore but as our Petty Cash. Maybe she'd used it for something and had forgotten to replenish it.

Andromeda the cat found me on the floor and curled into my lap. In Aida's absence, she yowled around the house like she did before she got spayed. She slept in Aida's bed next to her pillow as if Aida were still there, nestled under the covers. She purred against my knee, and I ran my hand over her back, but she stiffened and looked up at me, hissing and showing her teeth before running off, and I knew she, too, had mistaken me for my sister.

•

Aida and I turned sixteen a month before she disappeared. The other girls in town had lavish Sweet Sixteen parties in hotel ballrooms or in rented backyard tents. Aida and I didn't like those sorts of parties. We went when invited and sometimes danced, though Aida always got asked more than me. We were identical, with our father's bony nose and our mother's black eyes and wavy hair, and, as our parents called us, tall, dark, and Sephardic all over. But people only confused us from a distance. Aida was the prettier one. Maybe it had to do with her easy way. Her trusting smile. I've always been the skeptical one. Aida said this made me come off as guarded, aloof. It made boys afraid to get near.

We were both virgins, but she was ahead of me by her first kiss. She'd had it right there in our house during a party our parents hosted when our mother's jewelry collection got picked up by a fancy department store in the city. She could call herself a real designer now, not just a suburban hobbyist selling her chokers and cuffs at craft bazaars. One of her friends brought her stepson who'd just failed out of his first semester of college. Our father was trying to talk some wisdom into the kid, whose name was Marlon, and inspire him to go back. Later, Aida arrived at Marlon's side with a tray of crudités. For a virgin, I'd teased her, she had her moves. She brought him up to our attic cave, and he'd gotten past her lips to her bra before our mother noticed she was gone from the party and found the two of them unzipped on our beanbags. A minor scandal ensued. Our mother called him a degenerate pedophile in front of the whole party, and his stepmother said Aida was too loose for her own good. After all the guests had left, our mother sat Aida and me down at the kitchen table and warned us that the world was full of losers like Marlon who'd come along and steal our potential if we weren't careful, while our father just looked on from the doorway, eyes watery for reasons I will never know.

Neither of us was ever interested in the boys at school though. Sometimes we'd have innocuous crushes, like Aida's on the gas station attendant up on Hawthorne Avenue or mine on the head lifeguard at the town pool, boys who were just out of reach. Our parents had always told us we were better than the local boys: suburban slugs who, at best, would peak in their varsity years and come back to this town to be coaches or commuters. We, on the other hand, were sophisticated nomads, elegant immigrants, international transplants who spoke many languages. We had our mother's inherited Spanish, Italian, and quasi-British private school inflections, and our father's French and even a bit of his father's Turkish. The fact that we'd settled here was incidental, temporary, even though Aida and I had been here all our lives.

"You're not like them," our mother would say every time we were tempted to compare ourselves, asking for money to buy the latest fashionable jeans or shoes. "Don't ever think you are."

•

For our sixteenth birthday our parents took us to the Mostly Mozart Festival at Lincoln Center. It was a warm July night. During the intermission we went out to the fountain so our father could smoke a cigarette, and Aida and our mother drifted up toward the opera to look at the hanging Chagalls. I stayed with our father. I asked him to let me have a smoke too, like I always did, because it made him laugh, though he never gave in. But that night, even though we were supposed to be celebrating, he was somber.

"I don't want you to pick up any of my bad habits, Salma."

Sometimes our father put things out there, like he wanted me to push him to say more, but I wasn't in the mood. Not on this night.

I'd always been his confidant like Aida was our mother's. For a while now, he and our mother had been doing well, hardly any fights. Aida said the Angry Years were behind us. The crying, the oversensitivity, the accusations, the hysteria. Aida said our mother was too romantic for our father. He didn't appreciate her capricious moods and found them unnecessary. Aida said it had nothing to do with our father's affair, but something deeper between them and that our mother was too progressive to get hung up on infidelity. She'd found out the usual way when the girl, one of our father's students, called our house and told her she was in love with her husband and that he wanted to leave his wife and daughters for her.

I'd had my suspicions since the day our father was promoted to chair of his department and our mother decided this was our father's way of undermining her intelligence yet again. She'd locked herself into their bedroom, but instead of pleading to her through the door, our father went out to the backyard to smoke, and when I arrived at his side he looked at me and said, "Can I tell you something, baby?"

He only called *me* baby. Never Aida, whom he called darling.

"I don't love your mother anymore."

"Yes, you do."

He shook his head. "No, I don't."

I never told Aida. She thought she had our parents all figured out. When we later discovered love notes in his briefcase from his college girl, Aida said it was probably just a crush gone wrong. It would pass, she said, our parents were too old to leave each other and start new lives. They'd eventually accept this marriage was the best they could do. I let her have her theory. But I knew my father truly loved that college girl, even if just for a moment, and even if it had nothing to do with who she was but who she wasn't.

•

It was the end of the summer. Another week until I started eleventh grade and our father was due to go back to the university for the fall semester. Our mother said I didn't have to go to school anymore. I could be homeschooled, work with tutors, and spend my days in the house with her. Watching. Waiting. She hardly ate. She drank sometimes. Just a bit to wash down her Valium, which she hadn't taken in over a decade but one of her Manhattan friends showed up with a vintage vial for the rough nights. Our father didn't try to stop her. He was drinking and smoking more than usual too, as if with Aida gone we'd become short-circuited versions of ourselves.

I wasn't sleeping so much as entering a semiconscious space where I'd talk to my sister. Our mother believed someone was keeping Aida prisoner. In a shed. A garage. A basement. In a wooden box under a bed. I tried to picture her in her darkness. I knew wherever she was she'd be able to hear me speak to her in my mind. Our mother used to buy us books on telepathy. She said it was one of our special twin gifts. We'd play "read my thoughts" games in our bedroom every night. We learned to speak to each other silently from across a room and know what the other was thinking. In seventh grade, when Aida got a concussion from falling off her bike after skipping breakfast and dinner the night before, I knew it before the neighbor from across the street spotted her hitting the curb. I'd felt her fainting, her fall, the impact of the sidewalk hitting her cheek, the sting of broken skin and warm fresh blood.

I waited for the pain. Something to tell me what was happening to Aida. I tried to feel her. I wanted to make our bodies one again. Remember that her veins were once my veins and her heart was my heart and her brain was my brain and her pain was mine. I waited for the sensations. I wanted them to hit me, and within them I'd be able to know the story of her disappearance. I'd know who stole her. What they were doing to her. How they were punishing her.

I knew she was alive. Otherwise something in me would have signaled her death. If she'd been hurt or tortured or even killed, my body would have turned on itself. One of my limbs would have blackened with necrosis. My fingers and toes would have contorted, or my skin would have burned over with boils and cysts. I didn't dare consider the possibility that I could be like the starfish, a self-healing amputee capable of regeneration.

I heard the phone ring downstairs. Aida and I had our own line in our room, but it hardly ever rang. The family line never quit until night, when the calls cooled and our house fell into a cemetery silence. I heard footsteps and knew it was our father. Our mother hadn't been up to our room since the day Aida went missing, when she searched her dresser and desk for a diary, photographs, or letters. I think our mother was hoping Aida wasn't as good as we all thought she was. She foraged for evidence, anything that would give her a suspicion, a place to look. I watched her rummage through Aida's drawers and even accuse me of hiding things, but I told her, just like I'd told the detective, Aida didn't have a secret life beyond the one we had together under those lopsided attic walls.

Our father pushed the door open. I never bothered closing it all the way. His eyes avoided Aida's half of the room, and he settled on the edge of my bed. I was lying above the covers with my day clothes on even though it was close to midnight. I thought he was just coming in to check on me, since I hadn't bothered saying good night.

He wouldn't look at me, his chin trembling.

"They found her shirt." He folded over and cried into his hands.

I sat up and put my arms around his shoulders as he choked on his breath.

Later I'd hear her shirt was ripped almost in half and was found stuffed into a bush behind the high school parking lot. I, however, took this as a good sign. A sign that Aida was real again, not the lost girl in danger of becoming a legend, the girl the townspeople were starting to get tired of hearing about because it made them scared and nobody likes to feel scared. A ripped shirt meant she'd resisted. But it also meant she was up against someone brutal. The high school parking lot meant she'd been close to us that first night. So close we might have even passed by her when I went out with our father in his car to retrace her steps and mine and go to every familiar place. The school grounds were empty that night. I'd stood out by the bleachers and called her name. I'd felt a lurch inside my chest but around me there was only silence, wet grass, a high moon. On the ride home our father had driven extra slowly while I stuck my head out the open window hoping to see her walking on the sidewalk or under the streetlights, making her way home.

"We moved out here because we thought it would be safer for you girls," our father had said as if to both of us, as if Aida were curled up in the back seat.

We took a long time to get out of the car after we pulled into the driveway. Our father turned off the headlights and kept his fingers tight around the wheel. I wanted to tell my father it would be okay. We'd walk into the house and find Aida sprawled across the sofa just like last night when we sat around together watching dumb sitcoms. I wanted to tell him Aida had probably gone off with other friends. I didn't mind that she'd forgotten about me. My feelings weren't hurt. I wanted to tell him we shouldn't be mad at her for making us all worry like this. I wanted to tell him nothing had changed, everything was just as it was the day before, Aida guiding our family like the skipper of a ship through choppy waters, reminding us all to hold on to one another.

•

I didn't go back to school right away and never went back to my job at the coffee shop. Our friends came by less and less, and I understood it was because there was no news. Our father went to work, but I spent the days in the house with our mother. I followed the homeschool program and did my assignments with more attention than I'd ever given my studies before. Aida was always the better student. It took some of the pressure off. When I wasn't studying, our mother and I orbited each other with few interactions. Sometimes I'd suggest we do something together. Go to a midday movie or watch a program on TV. Sometimes I'd bring up a book I knew she'd read just to give her the chance to talk about anything other than Aida, but she never took me up on any of it. She spent most afternoons in a haze, drifting from bed to kitchen to sofa to bed, taking long baths in the evenings when I thought she might drown herself accidentally or on purpose. The people in town were still holding candlelight vigils at Memorial Park every Friday night in Aida's honor, but our mother never went. I went twice with our father, but we agreed turning Aida into a saint wasn't going to bring her home any faster.

The vigils continued though, and the volunteers kept searching the wooded areas around town, the shrubbery along the highway, the vacant buildings and abandoned lots next to the railroad tracks. The reporters kept the story in the news, and when her shirt was found, the TV stations wanted a statement from our parents, but they were too broken down to talk so our next-door neighbor whose dog once tried to eat Andromeda spoke on their behalf. The police wouldn't let me do it because they didn't want whoever had Aida to see me and know there were two of us out there.

Sometimes people brought us food. Casseroles, lasagnas, hero sandwiches. The church ladies dropped Mass cards for Aida in our mailbox. The department store where she worked set up a fund in Aida's name to help send some kid to art school, and there was a community initiative to raise money to contribute to the reward my parents had already publicly offered for Aida's safe return or information about her disappearance. Our father said we should be grateful to live in such a supportive and generous town, but our mother resented it. She hated that she was the one—the mother who'd lost the daughter. She hated that her life, which she'd curated so meticulously, had become something else. Her Aida was no longer her Aida but a story that belonged to all of them now. But our father didn't want us to come off as unappreciative, so he took me aside and told me I was in charge of writing thank-you notes and, on every note, I was to sign our mother's name.

•

Aida and I had a plan. After high school, we'd go to college in Manhattan. I'd go to one of the universities and study history, and she'd go to one of the art schools. We'd share an apartment and get jobs near each other so we could see each other for lunch or meet after work like we did here in town. We'd make extra money by signing up for twin research studies like we always wanted to do though our father never let us. We'd never live apart. We'd have to meet and marry men who could get along like brothers and tolerate our bond with good humor. If not, we'd be happy to live as a twosome forever. We'd move back in with our parents and look after them in their old age. It wouldn't be so bad.

Our mother liked to think she raised us to live in a bigger world, but Aida and I only wanted a world together. Our father tried to undo this attachment early on by sending us to separate summer camps, but Aida and I protested until they finally let us go to one in New Hampshire together. It didn't become a trend though. Aida and I figured out quickly that our absence had led our parents to the brink of divorce. When we returned, our father was sleeping in the guest room. I urged him to offer endless bargain apologies, for what, I had no idea, and Aida encouraged our mother to forgive, and after she was done forgiving, to forgive some more.

I often wondered how our parents survived six years alone together before our birth when they had so little in common.

"It's just love," Aida would say, as if that explained everything.

She always had more answers than I did about why things were the way they were, so one day I asked her if she would love me this much if I wasn't her twin, and she didn't hesitate before telling me, "It's *only* because you're my twin that I love you this way."

•

The night our mother caught her on our beanbag with Marlon, Aida told me that being kissed for the first time was like being stabbed in the chest. I said that didn't sound very nice, but she assured me it was; the feeling of being breathless and ripped apart followed by a beautiful hot internal gush. In the early days of her disappearance, our mother's suspicions had gone straight to Marlon. His father and stepmother lived a few towns over, and he hadn't yet gone back to school. The police looked into it. Marlon admitted that after their encounter he and Aida had called each other a few times, which I never knew, but he insisted they'd never seen each other again. He had a solid alibi for the night Aida disappeared in his stepmother, who said he'd been home watching television with her. As the months passed, our mother became obsessed with him, regularly phoning his stepmother to call her a liar and Marlon a monster until the lady filed a complaint and the police told our mother she had to stop harassing them or else.

•

Every now and then we'd get word of another sighting. Someone saw Aida in Texas the same day she was also seen in Seattle. There was a spotting in the next town over, down the shore, up in the Ramapo mountains, and out by the reservoir. The police followed these leads, but it all pointed to nothing. Even as the reward money increased, there was no solid theory for what might have happened to her. The locals started worrying maybe there was a serial killer on the loose, but that would suggest Aida was murdered—and there was no body. The reporters liked to say that for the missing girl's family the worst part was not knowing, but our mother always said not knowing preserved hope that Aida would soon come home, and hope is never the worst thing. Our mother warned the police and detectives not to use words like *homicide* in our house. Aida was alive. She might be half-dead, broken apart, mutilated, and, of course, she would never be the same, but Aida was alive, and unless the police could present her cadaver as proof, we were not allowed to think otherwise.

At dinner our mother pushed her food around her plate. We didn't bother nagging her to eat anymore. Her hunger strike was for Aida, who she was sure was being starved in some psychopath's home dungeon. Sometimes she had visions. She saw Aida chained to a radiator crying out for help. She saw her bound and gagged in the back of a van, being driven down some interstate far from us. She saw Aida drugged, captive in a dingy den, man after man forcing himself onto her.

Our mother never left home in case Aida returned after escaping her captor, running to our house, where she'd find the door unlocked, our mother waiting with arms open. Even at night, our mother insisted on keeping the door ajar. Our father told her it was dangerous, but she said she feared nothing now. Everything she loved had already been taken from her.

•

A few days into December we got the call that a hiker up in Greenwood Lake found Aida's boots. They were ruined from months of rain and snow, but the police took them for analysis. Just like with her purse, there were no discernable fingerprints, but Aida's blood was found in trace amounts. It could have been from before. A cut. A picked-over bug bite that left a smudge of blood on the leather. After all, our mother offered, Aida had that terrible habit of scratching an itch until it became an open sore. Or, the blood could have come after.

I slept with my identical pair of boots for weeks after that. I held them into my chest and closed my eyes waiting for images to burn across my mind, but they never came. I spent hours in bed staring at Aida's half of the room, still afraid to cry because I told myself you only cry for the dead.

•

That Christmas passed like any other day. The year before, Aida and I had helped our mother with the cooking while our father fumbled with the fireplace and played old French records, but this year there was no music and the three of us ate reheated food delivered by the townspeople. Our parents floated around the house avoiding each other while I divided my time between them, then alone upstairs in our room with Andromeda. Days earlier, a documentary-style crime show called asking if they could do a one-hour special on Aida's disappearance with family interviews and all. They assured us it wouldn't be tacky or macabre and said that in a few cases, their shows had helped witnesses to come forward with information about the disappeared. Our father had agreed, but when he told our mother I could hear all the way in the attic as she cried out, "What do they want from me? There's nothing left for them to take!"

Our father thought publicity would be good for Aida's case. The campaign to bring her home as if she were a POW was down to its final embers, and the detectives had recently come by to warn our parents with weak well-meaning smiles that there was a good chance we might never know what happened to her. They encouraged us to join a support group and gave us a list of networks for families of missing people. But our mother insisted that because Aida was alive, that kind of publicity would force whoever had her to cause her more harm or finish her off out of fear of being caught. She didn't trust the media, believing their stories on Aida were meant to sell papers rather than to find her. She regularly accused the detectives of incompetence, calling them village sleuths who never investigated more than a stolen bicycle and who secretly wanted to abandon Aida's case because it tarnished the town's safe image. She considered all the neighbors suspects. Every man who'd ever met Aida was a potential kidnapper or rapist, and every woman, a jealous sadist. It was a community conspiracy. It was because we were outsiders. It was because Aida was so perfect that people wanted to hurt her. It was because we never belonged here that they wanted to hurt us. Our father didn't disagree with her anymore. I wondered if it was because he'd given up trying to reason or if it was because he was starting to believe her.

·

I celebrated our seventeenth birthday twice. Our mother was finally willing to leave the house for hours at a time, so she took me to dinner at a Thai restaurant in town. For dessert, the waiter brought me a mango mousse with a candle jammed into its gooey surface. I smiled at our mother. I knew she was making an effort. She held my hand as I blew out the candle. It was strange to see her thin finger free of her wedding band.

When we walked back to the car, a group of kids driving fast down Elm shouted, "Hi, Aida!" They did this sometimes when they saw me around, whether it was a sincere error in recognition or just to torment us, I never knew. Our mother pretended not to hear them. She was getting stronger about these things.

That weekend I also celebrated with our father. He took me to Mostly Mozart again, and this time, he offered me a cigarette by the fountain. He'd moved out two months earlier. He swore to our mother it wasn't for another woman but because he just needed to be on his own, to discover who he really was. Our mother turned to him with a stare that was somehow vacant while containing the sum of her life.

"If you don't know who you are by now, my love, not even God can help you."

He rented a small dark studio near the university. It had an interior view, a Murphy bed, and a kitchen with no stove. It was all he could afford as long as he was still paying the mortgage on our house in the suburbs, and there was no way, as long as Aida remained unfound, that our mother would let him sell it.

He admitted to me that he'd been planning to leave our home since long before we lost Aida. He loved us, he said, but he always felt a misfit among us, out of place, as if he'd made a wrong turn somewhere. He said there was a time when he thought he and our mother would grow closer from the pain of Aida being gone but he was tired of trying and tired of hoping.

"You understand, baby," he said, and I was embarrassed to tell him I didn't.

"You're all grown up now. Only another year and you'll be off to college. There will be new beginnings for all of us."

We still didn't know how to talk about Aida. I asked him, because I knew he would tell me the truth, if he thought we'd ever find her or at least know what happened to her.

"No. I don't."

Just like our mother couldn't go on without Aida, I knew the only way our father could hold on to her was by letting her go.

•

Later that summer, some teenagers getting high up on Bear Mountain came across what they thought was a deer carcass and started poking around until they spotted a human skull. When the forensics results came back conclusive, the newspapers decided, as if they were the judges of such things, that our family could get closure now, find some peace in knowing the search was over, and Aida's broken, abandoned body could finally be laid to rest. The community held a big public memorial at the same spot in the park where they'd held all their vigils, but our mother insisted Aida's funeral service be kept private. And so, we sat on a single pew before the altar watching a priest who never knew her bless my sister's pine casket, the four of us together in an otherwise empty church for the first time since our tandem baptism, though our family was far from religious and, if anything, Aida and I were raised to believe in only what is visible.

A few days before Aida's remains were found, I walked slowly through the park on my way home from school the way I often did in a sort of meditation, whispering her name with each footstep, wondering what would become of us, what would become of me, all those empty years spread out ahead of us in which we were supposed to go on living without her. Across the brick path, I saw a pair of kids chasing pigeons and I thought of my sister, the way she would have walked over to them and explained with her boundless patience that it was wrong to scare helpless animals, they belonged to nature just as much as two-legged wingless folk did and had the right to live without fear of unreasonable human violence. And then I heard her call my name, loud, with laughter just beneath it, the way she would call to me when we'd meet each other halfway after work, her airy voice rushing through the mosaic of dried leaves on the wilting grass, shaking the naked branches overhead, then departing just as quickly as it came, leaving the park and every breath of life within it entombed in stillness. Anybody else would have called it the wind, but me, I knew it was something else.

FAUSTO

FAUSTO AND I WERE TOGETHER SEVEN YEARS BY THEN. THE NEIGH-
borhood people still called us los niños even though we were twenty-
five, not kids at all. We were at Virginia Key, the segregated beach in
the not-so-old days, and maybe it still is in some way because you only
see inland Colombians there now. It was August. We were fresh out
of hurricane number three. Our homes lost power, and because of
where we lived we knew it would be a few days before we got it back.
The hurricane pulled the seaweed out to the bay, turning the water as
Caribbean turquoise as Miami gets. Fausto and I splashed around and
made plans like we always did for when we got married, our honeymoon in Cartagena or San Andrés. Fausto wouldn't propose without
a ring though, and that ring was taking a while because Fausto wasn't
exactly making millions as a security guard. I was wearing the string
bikini he bought for me at some junk shop on Collins Avenue, and
when we were up to our chests in water I pressed my body against his.

"I don't need a ring, Faustito. No woman in my family ever got a
ring. Let's not break the tradition."

The sand was a brilliant white, but you can't stop sludge around here. I'd see guys on the side of the road selling piles of local catch shouting, "Fresh fish! Fresh fish!" and tell Fausto they were poisoning the community with those grease-bellied pescados. Fausto would say I was a pessimist and a paranoiac, but I didn't care. I always carried alcohol pads to wipe our feet so we wouldn't have to bring the ocean's caca home with us. I was wiping tar off my heel when Fausto started waving to this gringo in a suit like he was his long-lost papi and left me standing flamingoish on the hot sand.

I knew everybody Fausto knew, even the people I didn't know, like the ones from his job at the Diamond, a cylindrical Brickell condo that looks like a giant condom, because Fausto told me *everything*. He'd come home late, and I always saved him a plate from the restaurant, listened to his stories about los ricos, their hot cars and hot women, and how security guards are the eyes and ears of an apartment complex, know which residents are cheats, drunks, who gets visits from putas or cops. The gringo in the suit that day didn't look like anyone I'd heard of.

Next to the suit guy's fatness, Fausto was slim and brown, as if he'd been carved out of a coconut shell, swim trunks sticking to his thighs like cellophane.

I was still rubbing tar off my foot when Fausto returned.

"Who was that guy?"

"He lives in the Diamond."

"What did he want?"

"Just saying hi. What? I'm supposed to ignore the guy when he's waving to me?"

"What's he doing out here, in a suit?"

"Oye, Paz, you ask so many questions. Maybe he was checking the tide. How should I know?"

Fausto was one step from declaring me a pain in the ass, so I shut up. He did that a lot. An old trick that boys pull on their novias, calling them naggy nags to blame them for their scamming. Not that Fausto was on the cheater's track. No way. He relied on me too much for his babying.

He came up close to me, "Did I tell you I'm up for a promotion? Maybe this guy will put in a good word. He's on the board. They stick together, esa gente. And you know what that means?"

"What?"

"More money, honey!" He lifted me into the air by the force of his palms under my butt and spun me like I was a little girl even though Fausto and I were the same height, lanky, forever tan like chorizos. Same shoulder-length black waves that had everyone thinking we were twins until they caught us in a make-out. And the funny thing is we *could* have been related. Our parents were from the same hungry pueblo folded into the northern hills of Medellín. Maybe our abuelitas shared a lover. How else to explain that a continent and a few decades later we found ourselves looking into a mirror of Indigenous eyes, fat lips, touching each other's cheeks with identical square fingertips that the Twenty-Seventh Avenue bus-stop bruja told us were rare blessings, meant for counting money. Fausto and I always knew we were made for each other. Nothing could get in the way of *us*. Not even my papi, or his. So I didn't think much about the suit guy at the beach that day. Only about Fausto maybe getting promoted, getting that bigger pay-check, and finally buying a ring to mark his girl so the neighborhood would stop groaning that he was a loser. Fausto used to say that all this, the hurricanes, the beach, the boring jobs, wasn't real life—we were still in the womb and we'd really be born once we made some money, the kind of money where you don't have to worry about your car dying on the road, you can charge bags and bags of groceries, where you can pay all your bills and you don't have to buy crap at the flea market instead of a real store.

·

My father thinks people with natural-born money are evil, but that's because Papi got his start as a dishwasher. Worked his way up and now has his own cafetería Colombiana, so he's no longer broke, but he still talks like he is even though he just bought a brand-new Buick. And his restaurant doesn't have some supercute name like every other Colombian joint in town: Mi Colombia Querida, Mi Sueño Colombiano, Rinconcito Paisa, Casita Antioquia. No, his place is named after him, el patrón: Silvio's, the vain man that he is. I'm kidding. I just get on Papi's case because he was always on mine about Fausto, but really my father is a fine man and I love him. Anyone in our neighborhood will tell you I'm the best daughter on this side of the Caribbean. For example, I go to church with Papi not only on Sundays but also on First Fridays, some Wednesdays and Thursdays, and every Saturday, too, because Saturday is the day of the Virgin and if you go often enough, you might get lucky and die on a Saturday, and La Virgen will take you straight to heaven like a VIP. My mother died of an embolism when I was a baby. On a Saturday. Papi says she went to Jesus direct and he's repaying the favor by bringing the Virgin flowers every week. That's my father: Mr. Gratitude.

The church brought me Fausto, so I really can't complain. I was in my senior year at Our Lady of Mercy. Papi and I went to the Friday sunrise Mass. I don't know if they have those in other places, but San Lorenzo's parish is full of fanatics, so they make it extra for them. I received communion and prayed for a boyfriend, like usual. When we were headed home after the service, this off-duty priest, Padre Miguelangel—who was only a few years older than I am now and if he weren't a priest, Papi would probably beg me to marry him—approached us and said, "Don Silvio, I have a favor to ask you."

Papi loves when priests ask him favors. "Of course. Anything, Padre."

It's kind of funny when you see an old guy like my dad calling a newly minted priest *padre*. I personally had never called him anything but Miguelangel, even when he caught me crying in the back of the chapel after Saturno—the birth-control broker who supplied me and Fausto so Papi wouldn't find out—got busted for selling Mexican duds. The padre held my hand and prayed four straight rosaries so I wouldn't be premaritally pregnant, which we both knew would kill my father.

I never told Fausto. He was always saying San Lorenzo's is one big pickup spot.

"I'm going to send a young man your way," Miguelangel told Papi. "He needs a job. His mother is worried about him. His father died recently. Maybe you can give him something to do at the restaurant?"

"Of course, Padre. Consider it done."

"His name is Fausto. Fausto Guerra."

Papi chuckled. "With a name like that . . ."

Miguelangel smiled but caught himself and touched Papi's arm. "Just see what you can do for him," he said, then headed off to the rectory.

I was at school when Fausto made his first appearance at Silvio's. But when he showed up to start work the next morning, a Saturday, Fausto parked his body in front of my concession of vallenato and cumbia CDs, mochilas, bumper stickers, coffee, Colombian newspapers and magazines, and folkloric knickknacks.

He leaned against the glass case. "Who are you, belleza?"

"Paz. Silvio's daughter."

"And I'm Silvio, in case you forgot."

I didn't realize Papi had come up behind me. "Get to work, muchacho. You're an hour late."

Sometimes love hits you like a drunk driver on Memorial Day weekend. A tragedy, really, but you don't care because you're the victim and beyond hope anyway. I was lost on Fausto by the time he tied his kitchen apron and got to work washing dishes because Papi thinks cleaning is a purification of the spirit, and he'd test Fausto's humility before putting his pretty face to use as a waiter. I knew that was Papi's intention, but Fausto didn't last. It was only one week and six broken dishes till he quit.

•

I'd had visions of Fausto becoming Papi's right-hand man and Papi would give us the restaurant as a wedding gift and we'd manage it together and our children would work there and we'd start a chain of Silvio's restaurants all over Miami and buy a house on a canal full of furniture from Macy's. But Papi never got over it. Neither did Fausto. They only grew enough civility to nod at each other when Fausto came over to see me. Papi didn't let him sit at our kitchen table. Fausto ate his warmed-over dinners on the patio steps or, only if it was raining, hunched over his lap in the living room. He wasn't allowed into my bedroom either, but we got around that years ago when Fausto loosened the window frame so he could slip in from outside. Papi never set foot in my room anymore because I was a lady now. He's formal like that.

Fausto lived with his mom, la vieja Guerra, the world's most depressing exhibit of womanhood. A reclusive pygmy, always in nightgowns, never took the rollers out of her hair, hardly talked except to say, "Ay, Fausto," like he was slowly killing her or something.

"Ay, Fausto, I need you to go to Navarro's for my insulin."

"I'm going to work, Mamá. Ask Tadeo."

La vieja would shake her head. "Ay, Fausto. Ay, Ay, Ay, Fausto."

Tadeo was Fausto's weed-head slug of a brother, who, unlike Fausto, barely contributed a dime to keeping their mom from starvation or homelessness.

When I came around, la vieja treated me like Mother Teresa, because, I told you, I'm famous for being pious Silvio's dutiful daughter. I'd send her food from the restaurant through Fausto, and she'd thank me like I made miracles, saying, "Ay, Paz, your mami would be so proud of you," as if they'd been dear friends.

I only knew my mother through the living room photos in crystal frames and the family portrait from my christening Papi hung over the register at the restaurant. I hear she was a real saint, but people will say that about anyone who dies at twenty-six. Sometimes I wonder if she would have turned out like Fausto's mom, peeking out at the world from behind the iron bars of her house. Fausto's mother never went anywhere except to see the priests of San Lorenzo and complain about her troubles. Fausto's dad ditched them for a mistress and died in a mudslide. That was the official Guerra family story. The mistress part was true, but there was more, which Papi dug up through his blabbermouth church gang in his efforts to split up Fausto and me.

"His father worked for a narco," Papi said. "Why do you think he left the country? What idiot moves back to Medellín voluntarily? When he got out of prison, they deported him."

When I brought it up to Fausto, he looked like I'd knifed him. I loved him more than ever at that moment. I almost said so too, but he'd never believe me.

It happened in the early eighties. You couldn't make an honest deal in Miami without running into drug money. His dad was doing daywork in construction. I'd seen pictures. The guy looked like Fausto with an extra fifty pounds of muscle. A man came around his job site, a Coconut Grove compound, looking for guys to load trucks at some marina down south. They were offering big money and with la vieja, two little boys at home, and a mistress to support, he went for it. His luck, they were busted. Fausto's dad got eight years. His green card hadn't yet come through so he was deported on release, and they never heard from him again till word came that some kid shot him for his empty wallet.

"Why didn't you ever tell me?"

Fausto closed his eyes and rubbed his temples as if the memory gave him a migraine. I held him, kissed his hands and his face. We were lying on my twin bed with the pink canopy, which was pushed against the wall. My favorite place in the entire world because Fausto and I had to cling to each other all night to keep from falling over the edge.

•

Fausto didn't get the promotion. He didn't mention it until I asked. But then he grinned, and I knew there was something else he'd been waiting to tell me. It was midnight. He'd just gotten off work and come by my house for dinner. The air was thick with humidity, and we were sweating. Me in my shorts and tank top and Fausto in his polyester uniform pants and undershirt. He tore through his chicharrón. Only Fausto could eat a bandeja paisa for lunch and three chicharrónes for dinner almost daily and not gain an ounce. His face was smooth and glowed under the splinter of moonlight hitting the patio. I wanted to kiss him so badly but decided to wait until he finished eating.

"You remember that guy from the beach, in the suit? He gave me his card the other day and told me to call him, so I did, and he starts saying he's been watching me and he thinks I'm real responsible, a hard worker, and I keep my mouth shut. He thinks I'd be good at this freelance gig. He needs someone he can trust, and the money is tight."

"What do you have to do?"

"Nothing really. Just make some phone calls. That's it."

"Why can't he do it himself?"

"He's busy, obvio. I mean, the guy drives an Aston Martin."

"Why would he ask you and not someone else?"

He looked offended. "Not everyone sees me like your father does. Some people actually think I'm smart, you know."

"Don't be like that."

"You should be proud this rich dude thinks your man has potential."

"I'm always proud of you. I wouldn't be with you if I wasn't."

"You should be happy for me. Encourage me. That's what a good wife does."

"I am happy for you. But anyway, we're not married yet."

"Again with that, Paz? Fuck, you're always pressuring me."

"I'm just saying we could be married already, but we're not."

He shook his head like I was a disappointment.

"So who do you have to call, and what do you have to say?" I tried to sound cheerful, not suspicious.

"He's going to tell me more tomorrow. I'm meeting him at Bicentennial Park."

"Doesn't he have an office or something?"

"He's always on the go. With technology and shit people don't need offices anymore. Only viejitos like Silvio have closets in the back of the shop with fax machines and calculators."

"Why do you have to bring my father into it? He's a businessman too."

He laughed. "Silvio's is a garage with an oven. Soon as he dies and it's yours, we're selling it."

I turned away. Fausto had confirmed Papi's worst fear.

"I just mean we're meant for bigger things, Paz." He slid his hand on to my knee. "You could have gone to college and been something. You were a good enough student. But your papi makes you sell *I Love Colombia* T-shirts instead."

"It's an honest living."

"Listen to you! You sound just like him. *An honest living*," he imitated my father's heavy accent. "If you want to make real money, there's no such thing."

I hated when it came to this, me as Papi's ambassador, Fausto launching missile after missile, so I took his plate, now empty, and went inside to wash it. I'd go the inside route, then stop by Papi's room, poke my head in to say good night even though he was surely sleeping. By the time I brushed my teeth, my hair, and got to my room, Fausto would be in my bed, clothes peeled off, waiting.

•

The guy in the suit, whose name was Anibal—we never knew his last name—told Fausto to come up with one person who was reliable, had a clean record, an innocent face, a person who was discreet, preferably a girl because, Anibal said, girls come with built-in halos. Fausto, who thought of his brother, Tadeo, until he heard the halo thing, could only come up with one person. Me.

But I didn't know that part until much later.

I was at the restaurant when Fausto called. "Baby, I need you to do me a favor when you get off work. I need you to go to Wilfredo's Body Shop, pick up Tadeo's car, and drop it off for him at his new job."

"Since when does Tadeo have a car?" That was always his excuse for not having a job.

"He just got one."

"Where is he working?"

"That new mall. Biscayne and 145th. It's a black Bronco, and you're going to leave it in the handicap space in front of the liquor store and then cross the street, and I'll pick you up at the gas station."

"What about the keys?"

"Keep them. Tadeo has a set."

"Why the handicap? What if it gets towed?"

"It's just easier. Shit, Paz, if you don't want to do the favor, just say so. Why do you have to whine and interrogate me about everything?"

"I'll do it. I just want to be clear."

The body shop was a few blocks from Silvio's, so I walked. The place was already closed except for a young guy sitting on a plastic crate along the fence, right behind the car. I assumed Tadeo had called ahead because the guy pulled the keys from his pocket and handed them right over before I said a word. I was impressed. A sharp ride with tinted windows. Not bad for a guy who spent life glued by the culo to the couch, smoking yerba.

I drove up I-95, sampling the stereo system. Traffic wasn't so bad, and I liked the feeling of driving a tank of a car because my little bean of a Mazda rattled like a maraca on the highway. I left the car in the handicap spot and scuttled like Frogger across Biscayne. Fausto was there. Reliable, no matter what my father said, sitting in his black

Sentra with some old Metallica cassette playing. Usually he'd get out of the car to open the door for me, but this time I let myself in and when I said, "Oye, where's my chivalrous prince?" he fumbled with the volume knob and said, "Baby, this is a really good song."

He took the back roads home. I told him what a sweet car it was. I'd have to congratulate Tadeo next time I saw him, though we rarely crossed paths since I was always working and he was always home or out refilling his stock.

"We should get a car like that one day," I said. "When we get married."

Fausto smiled at me. "We will, we will."

"We'll pack up the kids in their car seats and go to the beach," I said, because I knew it would crack him up. Fausto had been dying to impregnate me since the end of our first date to the county fair. We had baby names picked out and everything.

"Soon, Paz, soon," he said, like he knew something, and for a second I wondered if maybe I was pregnant, but now we got our pills from Jorge, who worked at a real pharmacy in Doral, and I was super religious about taking them most of the time.

•

I didn't ask why the Bronco, a new car, wound up in repair shops all over Miami. And since Tadeo couldn't hold a job, no surprise, I was always having to drop it off for him at his new place of employment, which turned over pretty much every other week. I never complained because I wanted Fausto to see that just like I was always there for my father to go to church, to open or close the restaurant, he could count on me too. Fausto was mad appreciative. He'd meet me on the other end of the errand, greet me in the Sentra with a wet kiss, drive me home, and we'd do it like we were new to each other, at the beginning of things, instead of at the end.

He started buying me gifts like in the early days, when he was still trying to win me over, counteract the neighborhood chismes and my papi's disapproval. Back then his gifts were small but sweet—chocolates, candies, roses, an ankle bracelet, or a sexy bikini like the one I still wore even though the spandex was thinning. Now, the gifts were bigger, and part of me was grateful he'd stuck it out at the Diamond. They'd given him a raise, and there was the cash from the calls for the fat man. The extra money turned into fancy underwear for me and a gold crescent-moon necklace with a dangling diamond star. Part of me wished it were an engagement ring, but I never said so.

During dinner one night, Papi pointed to my necklace, "Where did that pendejo get the money for that?"

"He's got a good job now. Insurance, benefits, the works."

Papi did his one-eye squint. Annoying as hell.

"He's been going to church too." That was a lie, but you can't blame me for trying.

"¿Sí?" Papi laughed. "Why? Padre Miguelangel got a money machine?"

"Why are you always so skeptical of him? You're not the only decent man on earth."

Papi smacked his hand on the table. "I'm the father, you're the child. ¡Un poco de respeto!"

•

I'm going to tell you now so there are no surprises later, Tadeo's truck was packed with kilos and kilos of cocaine and I was running it from traffickers to distributors like maldito UPS. It wasn't even Tadeo's car. Tadeo didn't have a new job, anywhere. He was exactly where he'd always been, rolling joints on the coffee table, watching the Discovery Channel. Fausto didn't tell me any of this until one night when I decided to wait to see if Tadeo came out to pick up the Bronco from the handicap space where I left it. Instead of Tadeo, another guy got out of a car in another parking space, jumped into the Bronco, and drove off. I ran to tell Fausto it was being stolen, but he just looked at me like he knew.

This is everything: for every transport that Fausto coordinated, he was paid five thousand dollars. That money, Fausto said, was for us. *Us.* For the ring, the wedding, the house, the car, the babies. To buy our freedom from my father, from his mother. He never told me the truth, for my own protection, so that if I ever got pulled over by a cop I wouldn't know what was going on, and so that between Anibal and me, there was no contact or connection.

"That's the way it works," Fausto said. "These people keep the links in the chain separate so that nobody knows more than one other person." He was stretching it, he said, by being the one to pick me up every time. He should have had someone else do it, but he wanted to make sure I was safe. It was because he loved me so much, Fausto said, not because he didn't want to have to pay someone else for that part of the job.

My heart tried to measure his lies while my mind started counting.

I'd done these pickup-and-drop-offs seven times in three months. We were deep in November, the holiday lights had gone up all over the city. Five thousand dollars a run. That was thirty-five thousand. Where was the money?

"You're wearing some of it," Fausto fingered my necklace and the edge of my bra.

After we got back to my house and Papi turned in for the night, Fausto met me in my room and got on his knees. He lifted the dust ruffle and slid under the bed frame, reached far into the corner that hit the wall, and pulled out an old metal *Star Wars* lunch box. He guided me down by the hand beside him, and we sat cross-legged on the floor. He opened the lunch box between us. It was packed with wads. Thirty-two wads to be exact.

"We can't put it in the bank. They'll ask questions. It's safer here, but forget you've seen it."

"We can't do this."

"Just a little longer. In six more months we'll have a hundred thousand. We can do so much with that, Paz. Think of it."

I want to tell you that it took a lot more for Fausto to convince me, but the truth is, I couldn't take my eyes off the money. I pictured us taking our vows, me in a gorgeous lace dress, his tuxedoed arms around me as we danced at the reception. We would show everyone who doubted us that we'd managed to make a real life together.

•

There was a strip club around the corner from Silvio's, and sometimes the girls stopped in for take-out arepas or buñuelos on their way to work. I'd watch them while they waited for Mireyis to fill their order, wondering what kind of a conversation a girl has to have with herself every time she strips. Sometimes they'd pass by Miguelangel's reserved table in the corner and say, "Padrecito, una bendición, por favor," and lower their heads. He'd always give them a blessing because he wasn't the type to discriminate. The girls weren't necessarily beautiful; a few were borderline ugly, but they were made up like beauty queens in tight, tight clothing, fake tetas exploding from their tops. Once, Papi caught me staring and did one of his sneak attacks, whispering from over my shoulder, "If you ever take your clothes off for money, I will kill you myself."

I rolled my eyes. "Jesus, Papi."

"I know that's what you were thinking!"

Sometimes I think Papi was born a senior citizen. There was no point in debating stripping with him. How I thought we actually owed those girls a cut because half our lunchtime clientele worked up appetites from watching their routines and lap dances. Papi's theory was that fast money is dirty money and the fastest money a girl can make is with her body, but that's because most people think drug-running is man's work.

Papi also says money is like horse blinders and blinders are how you bring down nations. I won't lie; I wore mine like a Kentucky Derby champion. There were people all over South Florida doing the same thing, driving cars full of cocaine and contraband from garages to malls, and I'd look at the cars on the highway around me, wondering which ones were loaded. I had a spotty driving record in my Mazda and a few ways of talking my way out of tickets. Any Miami girl knows if you tell a cop the reason for your speeding is your boyfriend just dumped you or you caught him cheating, the cop will almost always let you go. That must be what Anibal meant about the halo. But in the Bronco, I was queen of the road and didn't get pulled over once. I started to think my Saturday Masses were paying off and La Virgen was looking out for Fausto and me. I was sure she wanted to see us church-wed, baptizing our kids, the whole package. The delivery scheme was God's plan, divine intervention, down to the hurricane that brought us to the beach and to Anibal.

Our delivery fee was small potatoes compared to what the big boys pulled in. It was nothing if you really thought about it. If we didn't make the runs they'd find someone else to do it. Some greedy lowlife who didn't have honorable dreams like we did.

We deserved this money. We were good people. All Fausto and I ever wanted was to be together. You can't get more honest than that.

With the wisdom of a few more years on me now I can tell you, if love is blind like they say, hope and faith are its deaf and mute cousins.

•

Seventy thousand dollars. We filled the lunch box and moved on to shoeboxes, turned my room into a vault but never bothered screwing the window frame back in. We also didn't think twice about spending twenty thousand in just a few weeks, telling ourselves it was our commission. Fausto hired some guys to give his mom's place a paint job, bought la vieja and Tadeo a new TV and living room set. Bought my father some vintage tequila. New dresses, a watch, and salon highlights for me. A Ninja motorcycle, car stereo, and a leather jacket for him. Dinners out. Tables at South Beach nightclubs that didn't let us past the rope just a few months earlier. A weekend in the Bahamas. Like that, twenty g's *gone*, and we were dumb enough to think nobody was onto us.

I tried to be charitable with our new fortune though, dropping hundred-dollar bills into the poor box, bringing a weekly bouquet of two dozen white roses to La Virgen, thanking her for her protection. Once, I ran into Miguelangel, who I remember looked handsome that day with his fresh crew cut. I could see why Mireyis and some of the waitresses had crushes on him.

"¡Dios mío! We only see flowers like that around here for funerals."

I thought he meant it as a joke so I laughed like it was funny.

"I was curious who has been leaving those bouquets."

I gave a dumb smile because sometimes that's a girl's best defense.

He held up his hand to block the sun from his eyes. Didn't walk away but didn't say anything either, so I pulled a rose from the arrangement and handed it to him.

"You can put it on your desk or something."

He took it and smiled. "Thank you. It's been a long time since anyone gave me a flower."

"I figured."

"Paz"—he petted the flower—"is everything okay with you and Fausto?"

"Never better," I said, because it was true, and because I sometimes suspected Miguelangel regretted being the one to bring Fausto and me into each other's lives. They'd only met a few times, and every time I mentioned Miguelangel around Fausto, he'd roll his eyes and tell me basta with the priest talk.

"Any wedding plans?"

"You'll be the first to know. So we can reserve the church and everything."

"Fausto's mother is worried about him. And your father is worried about you."

I laughed like that was a joke too. "Everyone's *always* worried about us. We're fine. We've always been fine. We always will be."

I got this funny feeling I should get away from him and slipped into the chapel like I had urgent prayers to deliver. But Padre Miguelangel walked into the chapel right behind me, and I felt him watching from the back row as I lay the flowers at the Virgin's feet and dropped to my knees to pray.

·

We never made it to a hundred thousand. We were on our way home from a drop-off when Tadeo called and told Fausto some police had just come by looking for him.

Fausto drove into a desolate lot by the railroad tracks, behind an old warehouse where not even a streetlight hit us.

"Call your father. See if they're looking for you too."

Papi was at work, but any time someone knocked at our house the neighbors would tell them they could find us at the restaurant.

"Where are you, Paz?"

"I'm out with Fausto. Just checking in. Everything okay?" My voice was shaky. I hoped he wouldn't notice with the noise of the dinner crowd behind him.

"Sí sí, todo bien. Say good night when you come home."

"I always do, Papi. Bye."

I sighed the longest sigh of my life and looked at Fausto.

"Nothing."

A train passed and flashed white lights across Fausto's face, his terrified eyes. We sat in silence a long time. I didn't ask questions. I knew he was still trying to figure it out.

·

The next morning, a Saturday, I went to Mass with my father. After the blessing, when the sunrise parishioners were headed for the door, Papi grabbed my wrist and said, "Why don't we stay for the Vía Crucis?"

He came to church without me some evenings and did the stations on his knees. It was a long time since we'd done them together. We were at the sixth station. My favorite since I was a kid. Veronica wipes the face of Jesus. I'd wanted to be like her. It took a lot of guts to stick up for Jesus when the guy was getting the shit kicked out of him, dragging the cross, people throwing rocks and stuff. That's what I was thinking about when Miguelangel came by, I assumed to say hello like he always did, since Papi gave him a free tab at the restaurant.

"Don Silvio, there are some police outside."

I thought Papi was going to hit the floor. He must have thought the restaurant was robbed or on fire. I'm sure he didn't expect Miguelangel's next words to be: "They want to talk to Paz."

The night before, in the darkness of his car, Fausto predicted it would happen like this.

Before I got out at the gas station where Fausto left me so I could catch a taxi home, I'd turned to him.

"I'll wait for you. Even if they arrest you and there's a trial and they give you ten years or more. I'll wait for you."

He touched my cheek. "You always had the patience of a cloud."

"We can still have everything we wanted. Get married. Have a family."

I thought it would be enough. Fausto always said the only home he ever wanted was with me.

"Paz, if I go away, will you come with me?"

"Go where?"

"We could go back. To Colombia."

"Our whole life is here."

"This isn't a life. It never was."

Normally I'd look to Fausto for all my answers about the world, but now I could only look to the train tracks, the shadows of rats running across them.

"Will you come with me?"

I used to play this game: whom would I choose if I had to decide between my father and Fausto? If they were in a duel, like I knew they wished they could be, or if Papi went through with his threat to disinherit me if I married Fausto like I'd been planning since the day I met him. Whom would I choose if I knew I'd never see the other again?

Maybe it's a twisted mental exercise, but I pushed myself because sometimes it's only in making hard choices that you know where you stand in life. Every time, I chose Fausto.

In the end, there was no real question.

"I can't leave my father."

He nodded as if he'd known it all along.

Because I knew Fausto like I knew my own reflection, I knew he would hide in his car all night, park behind Silvio's because that's the last place anyone would look for him. After sleeping alone, I would go to sunrise Mass with my father. Fausto would be watching as Papi and I left the house and walked to San Lorenzo's. I would feel his eyes on me all the way to the church steps. And then he would be gone.

•

The police questioned me on an iron bench under the willow tree outside the church. Papi watched from a few yards away, Miguelangel's arm wrapped around him as if he were a child, and I noticed, maybe for the first time, how life had shrunken my father. I played stupid the way I'd been trained, and the police never charged me with anything. Never treated me as anything but the innocent, oblivious girlfriend. About me, the neighborhood people said, "Poor Paz, taking care of her papi her whole life, giving her heart to a desgraciado junior wannabe narco. Que hijueputa vergüenza." In less than a breath, Fausto's last name became Shame.

•

Fausto went to Medellín. We know because he used Tadeo's passport, and the police traced his plane ticket to a local travel agency where he paid in cash.

"All for the money," said Papi, when things calmed down and it was just he and I at the dinner table, no covered plate on the counter waiting. "He lost it all. Just like his father."

For a while, Papi made fun of me, calling me the Widow because Fausto hadn't shown any signs of life since he fled.

It wasn't all for the money though, because he left me with it. I thought he'd creep into my room to get some for his escape, but he never did.

I counted. It was all there. But I couldn't touch that money.

I went to San Lorenzo's on the Monday after Easter and hung out in a pew after the noon Mass with my knapsack beside me, waiting for Miguelangel to change out of his robes. He came up the aisle in his black day clothes, and I met him by the baptismal font.

I looked around. Just some scattered old ladies praying.

"Can I talk to you?" I pointed to the confessional in the back of the church.

"You want to confess?"

I hadn't planned on it but decided I might as well. I'd confessed only once or twice since high school, when it was mandatory. I'd been inspired to go a few times but always preferred to hang with Fausto instead. This time I didn't bother sitting behind the screen, just on the chair across from the priest. I didn't remember any of the protocol, so I just started telling my sins, starting with disrespecting my papi, cursing, fucking, and lying, ending with the drug-running. I knew Miguelangel could take it. It was public knowledge his entire family was gunned down in a military massacre so, for sure, he'd heard worse. I swear, it's always the people with the shittiest luck who end up closest to God.

But even Miguelangel, who had expertise in counseling convicted murderers, looked shaken. I was relieved when he absolved me because that's always good insurance. Then I told Miguelangel to hold on a second, pulled the backpack in front of my feet, and unzipped it so he could see the cash inside.

"It's seventy thousand dollars. I'm going to leave it with you. For the poor."

His eyes bulged, and he gripped his chair's armrests.

"I know people come here when they're broke and desperate, Padre. Sometimes that's the only time they come."

One of Papi's favorite old village stories is of the famous loan shark who had a vision of La Virgen in his aguardiente, repented, and donated his counterfeit bill printer to the church. When things got hard, the local priest would crank out some fresh pesos for his flock just like Jesus multiplying loaves and fish. It was only when the priest was on his deathbed and people were writing Rome to sign him up for sainthood that he confessed the real source of his milagros.

I told Miguelangel how the priest fed his community when they were starving, helped them pay off debts, weddings, and funerals with his secret money machine while the people were convinced it was the work if God.

"And maybe it was," I said. "Maybe that's how God works. You never know."

"We can't use that money here, Paz."

The stained glass window made blue and red spots on his forehead. It made me smile a little.

"You can pull a few miracles out of this bag, Padre, don't you think?"

Miguelangel couldn't stop shaking his head.

I pushed the bag toward him.

"Make sure some of it goes to Fausto's mother. And Tadeo if he gets in any trouble. And the old people, especially the lonely ones with no family left that I see getting skinnier every week. And anyone else you think needs a hand."

You can't blame the guy for keeping quiet. A priest could get into serious trouble for accepting drug money on behalf of his parish.

But he did. So we're not going to call it that anymore.

Go ahead and add money laundering to my list of crimes because the only thing I wanted was to wash those dollars clean. It's been three years, and the only trace of it is that the audience at Mass has gotten a little fuller and there are more flowers at the foot of the Virgin if you're in the neighborhood and want to take a look. And if he ever calls or if the night comes when Fausto climbs into my window like I've been praying every day since he left, I'll tell him what we did.

THE BOOK OF SAINTS

LA NOVIA

My friend Paola had an American boyfriend who paid for her new breasts. She found him through an online agency that connected gringos with Colombian women. You had to send photos before you could be called in for an interview. Paola did it for the breasts. I admit I judged her for this. I want to say that when I sent my photos to the agency I was looking only for love, not surgery or money or a visa. But this is only partially true. I was twenty-five years old and had recently been abandoned by Anselmo, the married man with whom I'd been carrying on an affair since I was sixteen. He was my high school English teacher. I signed up with the agency because I hadn't yet found any other way to forget him.

I lived with my parents. They'd been married for thirty years. They have only ever loved each other. My mother took care of elderly people in their homes. My father was a luggage porter in a hotel by the convention center. I would have had an older brother, but he died of pneumonia at two years old, before I was born and we had a chance to meet. My parents kept a photo of him in every room of our apartment, so it was as if he were still with us, the perpetual baby. Sometimes I wonder if this is why I never wanted children.

My teacher was afraid of impregnating me. He already had two children and insisted on using condoms. I was a virgin until him. The first time was in a supply closet at the school. He seemed so familiar with the space that I wondered if he'd done it like this before, with someone else. He was not a young professor, the kind you see in films about such relationships. He was near fifty at the time. I was closer in age to his children than I was to him. But he was slender and soft-spoken, and he told me I was brilliant, which I knew wasn't true.

He led a school trip to Cali, and I begged my parents for permission to go. They could not afford the fees, so he paid for me, and I told my parents that I'd received a scholarship. I snuck out of the dormitory room I shared with two other girls and went to his room. I became pregnant on that trip, but he made me drink enormous amounts of aguardiente until I threw up and blacked out, and the next day I bled and bled and bled. It never happened again.

At the agency interview, the woman in charge asked what I was looking for in a man. I said he should be kind and patient and sensitive. She laughed a little. I added that he should have a good job and own a house and never have been married before. She nodded but asked if I was flexible about the never-having-been-married-before part. I said I was. She asked if I would be willing to move overseas for marriage. I said yes, though I hadn't really considered this. It would mean leaving my job. I was a cashier in a specialty paper shop during the day. At night I sometimes helped my mother with her elderly charges.

The woman wrote down my responses. She took more photos of me and said she would put them into her "book," though she meant her website. It was a directory where an American man who had paid a membership fee could browse women's photos and request three introductions. I asked her if I would get to browse a directory of men too.

"No," she said. "All you need to do now is wait. Keep yourself pretty, your nails painted, and your hair done. And wait."

EL NOVIO

I'm not a pervert. I have no criminal record. I don't smoke and only have an occasional beer, usually at my brother's house when the family gets together. I don't gamble, except when some guys from work organize a poker night about once a month. I don't watch porn. Only what's on the cable channels I'm already paying for, but not real hardcore stuff, so I don't think it counts. I go to church. Not a traditional one. This one is small, started by this hippie pastor. I like what he has to say, so I go—even to Bible study sometimes. My family are atheists. They say I joined a church looking for a woman. That's not completely false, but I didn't find one there.

I've been divorced twice. The first marriage was to my "high school sweetheart," as they say, but she left me after five years because she realized she prefers women. The second was to a woman I met at a bar here in Harrington. Now, *she* was a drinker. She fought mean and dirty, and the next morning she would want to have sex and I'd remind her of all the unforgivable things she'd said the night before, but she never believed me. She got my house in the divorce. I bought a new one. Smaller. Far from town and the highway. I'm not cheap, but I've always been a saver.

I manage a Home Depot, and one of our vendors told me about the agency. He'd met his wife, this beautiful Colombian girl, that way. I say *girl* because she was under thirty. I think that's the appropriate cutoff. I'd just turned forty and was looking for a girl myself. I'd never dated anyone from another country. My wives, and every girlfriend in between, were all from upstate New York with backgrounds similar to mine, rooted in the area for generations. They could have been my distant cousins.

To be honest, all the girls on the website looked really similar. Dark hair, except for the ones who dyed it blond. (I've been married twice; I know what dyed hair looks like.) Most wore a lot of makeup, which I don't care for. The first two girls I picked said they spoke English in their profiles, but when we got to emailing, I could tell it wasn't true, and I wasn't in the mood to be anybody's teacher. The third girl didn't have email. "Only phone calls," she said in her listing. On our first call I liked the sound of her voice. She put English sentences together slow and steady, like a young gymnast walking a balance beam. I liked that she was deliberate and thoughtful. It said something about her character. Maybe I was wrong, but that's what I thought then.

I flew down to Medellín two months later. This was after we'd sent each other several photos through the agency. Nothing dirty like people do all over the Internet. Hers were posed shots probably taken by her parents or friends: Sitting on a park bench. On the sofa near a baby picture she later told me was of her dead brother. All dressed up for a cousin's wedding. Mine were snapshots of me at barbecues at my brother's house, fishing on the river, standing in an aisle at work. I found one of me in a suit, but my second wife was in the picture too, so I cropped her out.

She wouldn't meet me at the airport. She said the proper thing was for me to meet her parents first. I came to her door with a bouquet of flowers. We sat around their living room. They offered me soda and coffee and small sweet things to eat. I was watching her the whole time, the way she helped her mother serve, how she touched her dad gently, like he might break. I wanted her to touch me with that kind of care. I took her to dinner that night. She wanted to go dancing, but I can't dance, so we just sat on a ledge in the Parque Lleras with the weird trees, and she said I could kiss her before I even worked up the nerve to ask.

WIFE

As a girl, my mother took classes in school to learn how to be a wife and a mother and how to keep a home. By the time I went to school, those classes had been removed from the curriculum, though some mothers paid for their daughters to take private lessons from ladies who knew not only how to keep a home but also more refined skills like how to eat at an international table, how to serve a menu of several courses, and how to sit with your hands in your lap, knees together and ankles linked. But I didn't go to any of those classes either.

Our wedding was a small affair. There were only my parents and a few relatives. It was a church ceremony followed by lunch in a nice restaurant—the nicest my parents could afford. No family or friends from his side came. He joked that they'd already seen him marry twice. When I didn't laugh, he said it was too expensive for them to travel to Colombia for a wedding. He said we would have another celebration when we returned to New York, and this way I could meet everyone he loved at once. But there was no such party. And it was months after I arrived that any of them came around to meet me.

I couldn't yet work in the United States, and he said I would never have to, anyway. He left me in charge of the household, which meant cleaning and making lists for shopping. We went to the market together on Saturdays. I could see he didn't yet trust me with money. He let me buy new sheets and blankets and pillows for the bedroom after I said I didn't want to sleep on anything his former wives had slept on. There were two empty bedrooms in his house. We filled one with furniture so my parents could visit, and the other he insisted we keep empty and waiting for a baby.

It didn't bother me to sleep with him. He was not thin or fat but somewhere in between. A soft belly. Slack muscles. But handsome in clothes. He grew a short beard sometimes. I didn't mind when he kissed me. Sometimes he asked me to be more affectionate. He wanted kisses as soon as he walked through the door. He wanted me to respond to all his touches with desire, to take everything as an invitation and promise of sex. When I wasn't in the mood, he would sulk.

"I thought Latinas were supposed to be more understanding about these things," he would say, and I would pretend I did not understand.

We fought from time to time. His temper was not too horrible. He never hit me, though he did lock me in the house a few times while he went to work. It had not yet occurred to me to run away.

I asked for a gym membership so I could keep my figure. It became inconvenient for him to drive me there and pick me up, so he allowed me to get my driver's license and bought me a new car, which was really an old car, but it was my car, and that was all that mattered. I would drive to the gym twenty miles away and stay there for hours, even when I wasn't exercising, simply to see and talk to other people. Some of these people were men who smiled at me and sometimes asked me on dates even though I was wearing a wedding band and the emerald-and-diamond engagement ring he'd bought me on his third visit to Medellín. I always said no to these men, but sometimes I thought about them after I returned to the house, so far away from everything, set on a yellowed field with a view of only more yellowed fields and some pale hills in the distance. It was nothing like Medellín, so green and lush, an accordion of mountains folded into one another; smells and sounds and laughter and voices everywhere.

He bought a computer for me and another for my parents so we could use video chat and avoid enormous phone bills. My parents cried each time they saw me appear on their monitor. I noticed them growing older. Every year I promised I would visit, but every year he told me it wasn't a good time. Sometimes I spoke through the computer with Paola. She had married, too, though not to the American who'd bought her the breasts. She'd married a Colombian, something she'd vowed she would never do; she said they were all cheats and made rotten husbands. She had a daughter. Sometimes she breastfed her as we spoke. Paola asked me to tell her all about my life, and I began to cry.

"Don't worry. It's not so much better here," she said as she held her baby close. "You did the smart thing in leaving."

She never asked me if I loved him. No woman would dare ask another woman that.

Once, I cried in front of my mother and father, and for a few moments all three of us wept together into our computer screens.

My mother regained her composure first, suddenly scolding me: "Get yourself together. You're a wife now. Don't let him see you weak."

When I left my family for my new married life, my mother gave me a book of saints she'd kept all my life beside my brother's portrait on her bedside table. She said it gave her comfort to read about the tragic lives of the martyrs. It made her own burdens easier to endure.

Sometimes at night, as my husband sleeps, I go into the bathroom, turn on the light, sit on the cold tile floor, and read my mother's book.

HUSBAND

She wasn't the most beautiful of the girls I had to pick from. I told her this once, because I thought it would make her feel special, knowing she had qualities that set her apart beyond her tits and ass and the same fat lips every other one of those girls had. She gave me this look like she could have hit me over the head with a shovel and buried me herself. Everyone thinks about killing their spouse at some point though. My pastor once told me that.

She won't come with me to my church. She says she's got her own, which is Roman Catholic, just like the one we were married in down in her country. It was allowed, since none of my other weddings had happened in a church of any kind, and the priest was willing to overlook my divorces. Sure, it's probably the same God and all, but Catholicism is just too much ritual for me. On Sundays I drop her off at her church and then go to worship in mine. She usually hangs around with the Spanish-speaking gang at hers for coffee and doughnuts afterward. They're mostly local gardeners and restaurant workers, lots of women and kids. I know a couple of the guys from Home Depot. After I pick her up, we go back home and I take a nap till she puts together lunch. We've got an easy routine. She keeps the house nice. I like that about her.

When I proposed, after I'd gotten the all clear from her parents, she asked me, with this worried look in her eyes, if I was sure I wasn't burned out on love on account of my two dead marriages.

"Are you sure you can love me?" she asked.

"Sure," I said. "I already pretty much do."

"What does 'pretty much' mean?"

Her English was good, but some things slipped past her. I had to explain it means "basically," "more than almost," and "mostly kind of." She still didn't get it. So I told her I loved her down to my bones, and she seemed happy with that. She'd been telling me she loved me since our second date. I wondered if it was because she didn't understand the weight those words carried, though she insisted she did.

She was browner than any girl I'd ever been with, and her private parts were even browner. Her nipples were like pomegranate seeds. She always looked kind of bored when we were fucking, but that usually turned me on even more.

In the early days, when I was just visiting her in Medellín, I would sneak her over to my hotel while her parents thought we were at dinner or the movies, and we'd bang like a porno—I mean, the light ones I've seen, not the heavy stuff. Then she'd get dressed and put on her lipstick, and I'd take her home, and she'd sleep in her little-girl bed in her little-girl room.

Sometimes I wonder what happened to that girl in the hotel room, if she was ever really that girl. My parents and brother and friends all told me before I married her that girls like her know the game of how to land an American sucker. They said she'd take me for all I'm worth. There are ways around that, I said. No credit cards or property in her name, for example. She's got her own bank account with a few hundred that I deposited as a wedding gift. I'm no fool. Not this time. But the original hotel-room sex—I thought that was real. She keeps asking to go back to Colombia to see her family, and sometimes I think we should go, just so we can stay in the same hotel again and resurrect that girl I so loved to fuck.

I'm forty-five now and have put on twenty or so pounds since our wedding. I tell her she's to blame, since everything she cooks comes with a side of beans and rice. Maybe it's so other women won't look at me. She doesn't act jealous, but I've always heard that Latinas are the most possessive, so maybe she just hides it well.

She doesn't know I've set up two cameras in the house so that if I feel like it, I can check in on her from work without her knowing. There's one camera in the living room that lets me see when she's loafing on the couch in the middle of the day, and another in the kitchen, because she's gained a few pounds these last five years, even though she swears she hardly eats till I get home at night. I didn't put a camera in the bedroom or the bathroom because I think that's crossing a line. I also put spy software on her computer so I can see what she's looking at, since I've learned from watching her on the cameras that she spends hours and hours on that thing. Now I know she's not just talking to her parents or looking at the Colombian news but searching for images and information on other cities, even looking at apartment rentals and job listings in Miami and Los Angeles and New York City.

It's okay. There's nothing wrong with wondering about other routes your life might have taken or could still take. Nothing wrong with having fantasies. I've got some of my own. Real detailed ones too. I don't share them with her, so she doesn't need to share hers with me. That's why I've never brought it up to her. It's not like she's cheating. No harm done.

One of my fantasies she does know about, because I talk about it all the time, is the two of us having a baby. I ask her when she's finally going to decide she's ready. She made me get her birth control pills after we got married. She says that's why she's gotten a little fatter, not because she's nibbling on coffee cake at two in the afternoon while watching Spanish courtroom shows. Sometimes I see her chub and pretend she's pregnant, that a baby is coming, and sometimes I think about throwing out her pills and telling her, "That's it! Done! No more pills!" But that wouldn't be right.

MAMI

My daughter and I share a birthday, thirty-five years apart. When I was pregnant with her, I often thought of the baby I might have had with Anselmo, my teacher. That child would have been fifteen. I think of him as a boy, lost to heaven like my brother. The year I turned thirty-two, my husband said his insurance would no longer pay for my birth control pills. To pay for them ourselves would cost a fortune, he said. I knew he refused to wear condoms, so I offered to have my tubes tied.

He looked horrified.

"What's wrong with you?"

I didn't answer.

But I didn't become pregnant at first, no matter how often he worked for it, finding energy I never knew he had.

It was more than a year before there were signs of her life in me. He was full of joy, and soon I was too, because I thought of this baby as all mine.

I had a premonition that he would leave me. Maybe it wasn't a premonition but a suspicion. And maybe it was partly my doing, because in many ways I thought I might be driving him to leave. I did not love him. Of this I was certain. I had loved him once, during our very first months together, but I think this was because I knew it would make him want me. Love is magnetic that way. My love for Anselmo had kept him gravitating back to me for years, even when he tried to tear himself from me because he said I was ruining his life.

Perhaps my love for Anselmo has never been undone and this is why I will never love my husband. He is good to me. He has chosen me over his family. I can see his mother is envious. I suspect she is partly to blame for the end of his other marriages. The few times she came over, when our marriage was still new, she followed me around the house like a hungry hyena, waiting for me to do something wrong. When I cooked, she claimed to get food poisoning. She picked at my husband's shirts and trousers and criticized the way I ironed them. She opened the refrigerator and cabinets and complained about the quality of the products I bought.

I heard her tell my husband's brother she couldn't understand how her son had married an "animal" like me. I told this to my husband, and he confronted her. She denied it, of course, calling me a liar—then asked why he'd been so desperate to find a woman that he'd gone to a primitive country and married a prostitute. This was enough for my husband. He showed his parents and his brother the door, and I never saw them again, though I suspect he still visits them on his own sometimes.

The prostitute thing stuck with him though. He asked me once—late at night in bed, when our heads were close on the pillows, though mine was turned to the window—if I had ever slept with a man for money.

"No. Have you?"

He laughed. "No." Then he said, "But *would* you?"

"No," I said again. "Would you?"

He didn't answer, and I pretended to fall asleep.

I wanted my parents to come stay with us for the birth of our baby, but he said we couldn't afford it. We had already gone to visit them last year and the year before that, and we had spent a lot of money setting up the nursery with new furniture and all the baby equipment he was sure we needed. When it was time, he came into the delivery room and held my hand, but when he tried to kiss me, I screamed into his face in pain. I didn't want him to watch the baby come out.

I made him promise to stay north of my spread knees. I didn't want him to see the tearing of my flesh. I couldn't think of anything more intimate.

When we brought our daughter home, he held her so I could sleep and brought her to me when she cried so I could feed her. He was peaceful and patient and kind and cared for me as I rested. He took time off work to stay with me. One afternoon I awoke from a nap and saw my parents standing over me. I thought it was a dream. They sat beside me on the mattress and hugged me the way they would when they came to say good night to me in my bedroom back in Medellín, in the only home I'd ever known until this one.

My husband brought the baby from her room and placed her in my arms, and I placed her in my mother's arms, and then she placed the baby in my father's arms, and we stayed together, passing the baby among us while my husband watched, still and quiet, and I was grateful to him for letting us be. I think now that I have never loved him more than I did in that moment.

DADDY

I'm not going to lie. I've thought about leaving her. For a few years I thought she couldn't have a baby, and that caused me to wonder what I'd loved about her in the first place. Some days, when life became even more ordinary than usual, I started thinking maybe it wasn't too late for me and I could divorce her and marry someone else. There are people who marry four or five times. It's not as rare as you'd think. I could go back to the same agency and find another young lady the same way I found her. She turned out to be trustworthy. She never even lifted a twenty from my wallet or pocketed the bills I left around the house as a test. She's honorable. Surely there had to be more women like her.

But then she got pregnant. I think I worked harder at it than her. I mean, I was near fifty. It took all I had to hammer into her whatever

I had left. But she carried the baby those nine months, so in the end we are more than even. She's a good mother. It's like she gave birth to her best friend. She whispers all day in that little baby's ear like she's telling her all the secrets of her life, and maybe she is. She insists on speaking Spanish to her, and I think that's a good thing. It will serve our daughter well when she joins the workforce. God knows the few phrases I've learned have helped me on the job. My wife wants our daughter to be able to talk to her grandparents. She talks about taking our child to spend summers down in Colombia. She doesn't know it yet, but the answer is: over my dead body.

We had a christening. By then her parents had come and gone twice: once on my dime, once on theirs. She insisted we invite my family to the ceremony, so I did, but nobody showed up. I stopped by my brother's house to ask him what the fuck, and he spoke on his and our parents' behalf, saying they weren't interested in having a relation ship with our child. They said my wife had never taken the time to get to know them, that she just wanted me all to herself.

"Isn't that how marriage is supposed to be?" I asked my brother.

"You should know," he said. "Maybe we'll get along with your next wife better."

I've never told my wife about these interactions. She doesn't need to know. It's hard enough for her to deal with people in town looking at us funny, and when she gets pulled over by a cop for going over the speed limit on the highway, or even for no reason at all, they always ask her for her green card. She's a citizen now. Her English, as she would tell you, is "pretty much" perfect. Still, when she goes out with the baby in the stroller, she's regularly mistaken for the nanny—as if we could afford one. My wife mutters in Spanish after these incidents. I can make out a few words, such as "rosado como un marrano"— pink like a pig. I'm pretty sure she's talking about whatever white person offended her that day, and I hope to God it's not me.

I was certain she was going to fall into some kind of depression after the baby was born and her parents had gone home and I was back at work and she was alone in our house with a crying, hungry, fussy child on her hands. She can be an angel, our baby girl, but she's also got a devil in her and pipes that turn our house into a cathedral of screams no matter the ways we try to soothe her.

She's been baptized now in both our churches, so I'm sure she's not cursed or possessed and is just being a normal, natural baby. I'm getting older now, and maybe all of this is harder on me than I want to admit.

I'm still pushing for a second kid. I'll take another daughter, no complaints, but every man wants a son. My wife sometimes says she wouldn't know what to do with a son. She says men are born to wound. I don't know how to take comments like that, so I keep quiet. Then, after a good, long block of silence, I go over and tell her she will be a fantastic mother to whatever kid shows up in her womb, and she sort of smiles, and I kiss her face and her hair and finally her lips, and she lets me.

MUJER

All the pigeons had died. I had taken my daughter to the Parque Lleras in Medellín, where I used to go with her father, where I went with Paola and with Anselmo when we were still pretending to be only teacher and student, practicing English over an ice cream. At the park, my daughter and I saw feathers all over the ground but no birds, and no old people with little sacks of birdseed waiting for a flock to feed. I asked a woman on another bench where all the birds had gone, and she explained that it was a local tragedy: the caretakers had used a new kind of fertilizer on the gardens, and the poisonous runoff had killed all the birds.

My daughter's Spanish wasn't fluid enough to catch everything I'd been told. So she asked me again where all the birds were, and I found myself lying to her, saying they'd gone on vacation to visit their grandparents, just like we'd left our home in New York to come to

Colombia so she could see her abuelos. My daughter accepted this. I felt ashamed for taking advantage of her gullibility.

We had flown down to Medellín together a few days earlier. It was my daughter's first trip, and I'd wanted to show off my country, prove it could compete with the only one she knew. She had a terrible attachment to that American house surrounded by fields. Whenever we went beyond the town limits, she cried to go home. She wasn't even impressed by the beach, or the mountains, or Niagara Falls. She only wanted to be in that stupid house. I'd been bragging to her all her life about Medellín's permanent sunshine, the rivers of flowers, the sweet air, and delicious food. The last time I'd tried so hard to entice someone was when I'd met her father.

When he arrived to meet us two weeks later, my husband insisted we leave our daughter with my parents and stay in a hotel. He said we needed the time alone together. He said it could be like the honeymoon we'd never taken, since he'd spent all his money on his trips recruiting me to be his wife. In the hotel room we made love several times, though my husband seemed more tired than usual. My mother had warned me a man ages rapidly after fifty, and this seemed to be the case for my husband, but I said nothing, not wanting to make him feel bad.

He was especially quiet. I wondered if he was keeping something from me. I had no reason to suspect another woman, but I began to regret leaving him alone in New York. Then I remembered I wasn't even sure I loved my husband most of the time, and this made me think of Anselmo.

As soon as my husband's plane was in the sky, headed back home, I left my daughter with my mother and told her I was going to the store. I found a quiet alleyway between two buildings and called the only number I had for Anselmo, the one I'd memorized years ago and had dialed many times since from the United States, only to hang up before the first ring. This time I waited. I heard his voice, sounding so much older.

I asked him to meet me at the same hotel where I'd been with my husband. We got a room together, which I paid for in cash. For a while, we only watched each other. He'd heard I married an American and moved to New York. I told him I had a daughter. His children were grown. He was a grandfather. We kissed, then started to remove our clothes, but something stopped me. I put my clothes back on and told him I had to get home to my family.

HOMBRE

I gave up smoking twenty years ago, mostly because they made a rule against it at work and I got sick of having to stand out in the cold just to light up. I've always been in good health. Never a trace of a smoker's cough. I thought my aches and pains were just symptoms of old age. Arthritis runs in my family. The last thing on my mind was cancer.

They said it started in the lungs, maybe from the smoking way back when. Or maybe it's all the chemicals and crap I'm exposed to at my job, or the dust and paint I breathed when I was younger and worked construction, before all the current safety rules about masks. The doctor said there's no point looking for the cause when it's already moved well past my lungs and settled into my bones. Stage IV. Bad, to be sure, but not necessarily short-term lethal.

They put me on an aggressive four-week chemo regimen, followed by four weeks off, then another four weeks on. The doctor had to disclose that sometimes people don't even make it through the treatment, but he said my odds were good. And miracles do happen. Everyone knows that. My wife and I have got people in both our churches praying for me.

Our daughter is in school already, so my wife can take me for my treatments and get me home in time for the school bus drop-off. There's not much for her to do at the treatment center but sit with me and hold my hand. Even that hurts sometimes. Overnight my voice became this faint, scratchy croak. It hurts to talk. So my wife does the talking for both of us. She makes plans for trips we can take when I'm better. Her new thing is trying to convince me to buy a house for her parents in Medellín, someplace we can retire to when we're older. I tell her yes, anything she wants.

I'm glad I let her get a driver's license back when I first brought her to this country. She's been saving my life. She's the one who told my family I was ill. If it were up to me, I'd have left them in the dark. And if I'd gone ahead and died, I'd have enjoyed watching their guilt and grief from above. But my wife went behind my back and told them to come over, so I was stuck on the sofa, with a puke bucket next to me, watching my soggy-eyed mother kneel beside me like I was already half dead. She wasn't apologizing for anything. Instead, she acted like she was the one forgiving me for being sick. Then she told my wife to make us some tea, and I said, "Jesus Christ, Ma, she's not the goddamn maid!"

They were strangers to our daughter, and I didn't make any effort to warm things up between them when they were introduced. My mother told our daughter she was her grandmother, and our daughter responded that her grandmother was in Colombia, and my mother looked kind of devastated, but I was not at all sad for her. My brother just watched the whole scene: me sick as shit, and this strange reunion, his arms crossed like logs against his chest, his mouth screwed tight like an anus.

"Fuck that guy," I told my wife as soon as he was gone. "Fuck them all."

My wife said the medications were probably making me extra cranky. Our daughter was playing with her dolls on the floor beside the sofa. Every now and then I'd feel a doll walking up my leg. I dozed off, and when I woke up, there were dolls and stuffed animals all over me, and my daughter was at my side, watching me.

"Are you and your friends here for my funeral?"

"No, Daddy. We're here for your birthday party."

And then I saw my wife coming through the archway from the kitchen, balancing a cake on a tray, candles lit, tiny orange flames swaying like feathers plucked from some poor dead tropical bird.

They were singing, "Happy Birthday" and "Cumpleaños Feliz." My wife. My daughter.

"I'm so happy," I told them, my eyes misty as my wife set the cake on the coffee table and helped me sit up, and the dolls and stuffed animals tumbled onto the sofa cushions around me.

My daughter climbed into my lap. "Con cuidado," her mother told her. "Be careful with your daddy."

"I'm so happy," I said again and again, but they were singing once more and couldn't hear me.

CAMPOAMOR

NATASHA IS MY GIRLFRIEND. SOMETIMES I LOVE HER. SOMETIMES I don't think of her at all. When I met her she had a broken leg. I was visiting my friend Abel, who sells mobile phone minutes and lives down the hall from her in a building behind the Capitolio. I heard her crying, calling for anyone. I thought it was an old woman who'd fallen, but when I pushed the door open I saw a girl, maybe twenty-five, standing like an ibis on one leg, leaning on a metal crutch, her other leg bent and floating in a plaster cast. The stray crutch lay meters from her reach across the broken tile floor.

She looked angry even though I was there to help her. I stepped into her apartment, saw she was alone, picked up the crutch, and handed it to her. She slipped it under her arm and thanked me. I asked her how she got around. Her place was on the fifth floor, and there was no elevator.

"I've been up here for two months."

"Alone?"

"My mother lives here, but she works during the day."

I asked her name, and she told me Natasha, embarrassed the way we of our generation are to have Russian names.

"It's okay," I told her. "My name is Vladimir."

When I returned a week later to buy more minutes for my phone from Abel, I knocked on Natasha's door and it cracked open. Later she admitted there was no lock and no money to buy one, so at night she and her mother pushed a dresser in front of it. She was sitting on a sofa with mahogany legs, upholstered in a ripping flesh-colored silk, bulges of cushion tissue and bone frame exposed. Her casted calf was propped on a pillow mound atop the glass coffee table. She sat surrounded by books and said she only ever got up to go use the bathroom and to make herself something to eat.

"Don't you get lonely up here, Natasha?"

She shrugged.

"How did you break your leg?"

"It was stupid. Un mal paso. I was dancing with a bad dancer. He made me slip."

I was standing so she had to look up at me, trying to decide if she should let herself smile.

"I'll come and see you again," I told her.

She said nothing, but I could see in her eyes that she liked the idea. And so I kept coming, every time I needed a new phone card, and sometimes in between, and Natasha would invite me to sit on the sofa beside her and would offer only a few sentences. I could see she was depressed in that dark apartment, subject to the shadows of the Capitolio and the noise of its endless restoration, drills and hammers on stone, with not even a television to keep her company because theirs had burned out years ago and there was no money and no man to take it to be fixed.

I asked Abel what he knew about her. He's a writer like me. We met at the university where we both studied journalism. Abel writes small pieces for *Granma* and for an anonymous underground news-paper that gets published on USB sticks and passed around Havana once a month. He also sells black market phone cards. He says I need a side negocio. I don't even have a government job. This is why I never have money.

"If I get a job, I won't have time to write my novels," I say.

"What novels, Vladi? You haven't written even *one*."

Abel said Natasha had an older sister who died from an infec-tion and a father who left for Santo Domingo and was never heard from again. Her mother works as a cashier at the Carlos Tercero shopping center. He said Natasha reads a lot of books, though she didn't study in the university, and until she broke her leg she had worked as a niñera taking care of the children of a military family in Cubanacán.

"What about the guy she was dancing with when she broke her leg? Was he her boyfriend?"

"¿De qué hablas, Vladi? She wasn't dancing. Nata never goes out with anyone. She broke it when she fell down the stairs. A neighbor found her on the landing between the second and third floor."

•

Natasha didn't have anyone to take her to have her cast removed, so I offered. We left her crutches at home, and I carried her down the stairs all the way to Dragones for the botero lines. We found a shared taxi going down Zanja in the direction of the clinic and sat together in the back of that green Ford, our legs pressed together as other passengers climbed in beside us. It was somewhere around La Rampa that I decided I wanted to kiss her. We passed Coppelia, and she looked out the window, past me, licking her lips, saying when she could walk on her own she'd go there for her first ice cream of the summer. I kissed her mouth. The woman on Natasha's other side looked away. The driver watched us from the mirror. Natasha's lips were still, but she didn't pull away. I kissed her many more times, and when I paused she stared at me, but we were quiet until we arrived at our stop, and again I carried her, from the road and into the clinic.

When the doctor liberated her leg from the plaster, it was pale and thin compared to her other calf, which was golden and muscular. Natasha was embarrassed. The doctor made her practice walking. She was uncertain and wobbled and held my arm tight. The doctor said she had to be careful. Her ankle would be delicate for some time. She should not walk on Havana's cobblestones and uneven roads alone, he said.

"You take care of her," he told me as we left that day.

Natasha held my arm like a security bar, and I watched her every step in and out of the taxi back to the Capitolio. When we came to her building, she walked on her own to the corner in front of the Teatro Campoamor where some men were stealing sheet metal from the barricades.

"Let's go in," she said, and I followed her, because I was just meeting this Natasha of enthusiasm and with wildness in her eyes.

We walked past the street thieves, the walls of garbage, and into the theater through a gap that had been ripped through the wooden door blocks. Everyone knew a famous eccentric squatted on the theater's upper floors. From Abel's apartment you could see the guy's laundry hanging from string across what used to be theater balconies. Natasha led me in, and we were at the base of the old theater's concrete horseshoe, overgrown with plants, even trees, and I thought of my grandmother's old stories about the place, where she'd come to hear her first zarzuela when Havana was still grand and beautiful, before its shredding and abandonment and exodus.

Here, the balconies were lined with pigeons, and the orchestra seats, long looted, were occupied by a clan of bony cats. Natasha, still holding me for support, slipped both her arms around me, pressed her chest against mine, and kissed me. We were there so long I managed to lift up her shirt and slide my hands under her skirt and into her panties, but then we heard voices from somewhere in the theater and Natasha lost her balance, so I helped her cover up and took her home.

•

I have another girlfriend name Lily. She lives with her daughter in the apartment her husband left them in three years ago, in the building next to mine just off Línea in Vedado. I live with my parents. They didn't see the point of having more than one child. They didn't have the room for a bigger family. They sleep in the one bedroom in our apartment. I sleep on a mattress in a corner of the living room that my mother also uses to give therapeutic massages to private clients though she was educated in Moscow to be a physicist. My father is a cardiologist. He's hoping to get sent on a doctor exchange to Angola or Brazil so he can defect and get us out of here.

Lily doesn't care for books. She thinks it's funny that I want to write them. She wants to fuck almost all the time, even if her daughter is in the next room, and even if her daughter walks in halfway through because she's hungry, Lily doesn't want to stop. She got sterilized, so she says she's making up for all her condom years. She's thirty-five. I'm twenty-seven. Lily's face is hard from sun and smoking Hollywoods, and her hair is thin and limp like thread. Her body is lumpy; her stomach, a rumpled pillowcase. Somehow she's still beautiful. Sometimes even more beautiful than Natasha, who is lean and pointy, sharp shoulders, elbows, and hips, a smooth face as if carved of clay. Sometimes when I'm with Lily, I miss Natasha desperately. Other times I get a feeling of revenge. I speak to her in my mind as I lick Lily's body and say, *You see, Nata, you don't own me after all.*

I am with Lily when Natasha thinks I am writing. This is why she doesn't call or come looking for me. She wants me to be productive. I don't even have to convince her to give me the time and space. She read some pages I wrote a long time ago even though I said they were new. She thinks I'm talented. She believes I can be a great writer. I told her the novel I am writing is about love and mystery and the agony of existence. In my mind, my book is all these things, but the truth is I haven't written more than a few sentences. Natasha says it will be the greatest novel ever written. She says they will publish it everywhere and I will be invited around the world to talk about it and be given medals and honors and will meet important people who will think me brilliant. I have already told her I love her, so I know she thinks she will be coming with me on all these journeys.

Natasha has no money for books, but she is friends with all the dealers at the Plaza de Armas who let her borrow their used copies for a week or two, and then she returns them with a smile and a pastry or a candy or even just a kiss on the cheek. They like Natasha because she will sit for hours with them in the shade of the plaza and talk about Barnet or Padura and tell them the man she loves is also a great writer and one day soon his novel will be the most sought-after title on the island.

Here in La Habana Vieja, with her newly borrowed books tucked into her bag, Natasha is tough, confident of her steps, no longer afraid she will twist her ankle. When a shirtless boy of ten or eleven approaches her slowly, eyeing her, then, just as they pass each other on the sidewalk, the boy reaches behind her and slaps her ass with an open palm, Natasha is quicker than he anticipates, grabbing his wrist before he can run off, holding him in place as he kicks and tries to flee. But Natasha slaps him with her free hand, demands to know where his mother is, and vows not to release her grip until the little cochino takes Natasha to his mami and confesses his crime. Here, Natasha doesn't need me.

Lily doesn't have to work because her husband sends money from Tampa. He works for a moving company and is saving to bring Lily and her daughter over or maybe just enough to come back and live better. Sometimes she gives me a bit of fula, and I use it to take Natasha out. We go to Coppelia, wait on line for whatever disgusting flavor they have that day. Sometimes we go to a movie at the Yara or to Casa de la Música and Natasha presses close against me in the crowd as we watch a band perform. Then I take her home, and while her mother sleeps, Natasha sneaks me into her room. She always pretends she's making a great sacrifice by taking me to bed, like she's an angel and I'm a devil, not like she's enjoying it, though she doesn't hide her faces or conceal her moans. But she makes me work for it every time. Not like Lily, who never wears underwear, who doesn't have to be convinced of anything.

"When are you going to let me read your book?" Natasha asks every now and then when we are in bed together. It's enough to make me want to get up and leave.

"You know I'm a perfectionist. I don't want anyone to see it until it's ready."

Her friend, who works at a papelería, stole some notebooks for me because Natasha asked her to. I don't have a computer. Not even a typewriter. I had one, but the ink ribbon ran out and I can't find replacements anywhere. I write in notebooks. Natasha thinks I have dozens full of my writing, but it's more like three or four. In my mind I see stories I want to write, I hear the sentences, see each phrase come together like pearls on a string, but when it comes time to write them, they evaporate, and I'm left in the four corners of my room, my mother working on some bare body under a towel; or I'm in Lily's apartment, her daughter talking to one of the dolls her father sent from Florida; Lily, cooking a meal, humming some old tune, smelling of me under her clothes. If I were a better writer, a *real* writer, I would know how to make Natasha or Lily my muse. But I can't even do that.

•

Natasha's mother is small and fat in the way of most mothers around here. My own mother has stayed thin by kneading people's bodies all day, and my father hates this because he says people think he can't afford to feed her, which is mostly true. He earns too little. It's mamá's job that lets us eat beyond the Libreta de Abastecimiento, buy imported food at the markets, African fish and Chinese chicken. Natasha's mother is shaped like a frijol, with curly hair dyed tomato red, a woman who looks like a meal.

She tells Natasha not to read so much. She tells her that instead of babysitting, she should work on seducing one of the husbands who employ her so that she can blackmail him into sending her away to Miami or Madrid. Natasha can't help confessing these things to me. In the beginning, I could hardly get her to speak, but now I can't keep her quiet. She wants me to know all her secrets. I hush her with kisses, try to silence her with caresses, opening her legs, letting her feel me, but she wants to talk, every time. I tell her I love her, but that sometimes only fills her with suspicion.

"How can you love me when there's still so much you don't know about me?"

"We don't need to know everything about each other, Nata. I love the you I know."

This is the wrong thing to say.

"What do you mean there are things we don't know about each other?"

Nata thinks herself too intellectual to be jealous, so I know she won't allow herself to ask me about other women since I've given her no evidence.

"We have our whole lives to discover each other," I say. "But we only have an hour until your mother gets home from work."

Natasha's mother thinks I'm too poor for her daughter. But she likes that I come off as ambitious. Writers and artists and musicians can do well for themselves in this country if they make a name abroad. That's what Natasha tells her mother. I'm going to be famous, and Nata is going to be my pillar and raise our children. Just as soon as I finish my novel we will get married, she tells her mother. That line came from me.

•

Once, my mother said, "I don't think I approve of you having two girlfriends like you do."

"Why not?"

"Infidelity is an antiquated model, Vladi. One shouldn't be so greedy. Just pick one."

"I wouldn't know which one to pick."

"That's easy. Pick the one without a husband."

Later that night, as my mother soaked her tired body in the bath and my father washed the evening's dishes, I asked him if he'd always been faithful to my mother in their thirty years of marriage.

He looked at me as if I'd done something terrible of which I should be very ashamed.

"Never ask a man a question like that."

But later he came around to my corner as I lay on my mattress staring at the ceiling, my notebook beside me, turned to a blank page, and stood over me.

"The answer is yes."

He paused, looked around the room and back at me. "Do you believe me?"

"I will if you want me to."

"It's the truth."

"Okay, viejo. I believe you."

•

It has been years, but they say the end of the Capitolio restoration is in sight, the national assembly will soon be able to move in, and the Cuban government has decided to buy up the properties of those living around it for the purpose of creating more government office space. This is what the officials said when they came to see Natasha and her mother about being relocated. The compensation would be generous, they said. Fifty thousand dollars generous. I couldn't believe it. Until last year, one couldn't even buy or sell their own house, and now the government is playing real estate games? But Abel's family got the same offer, and the other families in the building too.

"Fifty thousand dollars is more than a person can earn in a lifetime in this country," Abel says. "Where do you suppose the government is getting all that money?"

"Who knows? Will you take the offer?"

"We don't have a choice. When the government says you go, you go."

Nobody has figured out Abel is the one who wrote the article for the USB newspaper telling everyone the American prisoner was being held in the back of a green house in Marianao next to Ciudad Libertad, right where Batista himself fled Cuba forever. He got that info from a neighbor who befriended one of the guards, who said they were treating the old guy pretty good because he would be the ticket to get the Five Heroes back to the island, and that's exactly how it happened. Abel scooped everyone.

Natasha's mother cries at the thought of leaving her home. We leave her to her tears and walk down to the Campoamor, where we still like to go to be alone though we're not really alone because of the pigeons and cats and people who hide away in its mezzanine corners even while blocks of concrete fall off the walls and ceilings.

We sit together near what used to be the stage, where great performers once sang, where elaborate sets were built and intricate costumes were worn. Natasha's leg has grown supple, and her ankles are almost identical in girth when I measure them with my fingers.

Here in the Campoamor she is again that girl of the ripped sofa, who looks at me as if I pulled her out of darkness. Not the hard-edged girl I see walking on the street when she thinks she's alone and doesn't know I'm watching.

Here in the Campoamor I love only her.

She starts another one of her confessions. How her mother used to scold her for not going out enough, saying she'd never meet a nice man that way, would never get married, and would die alone in that apartment by the theater. Her mother said she had to get out into the world; the man of her dreams wouldn't just show up and knock at her door.

"And look what happened," Natasha says, "Mamá was wrong."

I kiss her. But Natasha has more to say.

"Vladi, what if I didn't have a broken leg the day we met? What if I were paralyzed? Would you still have wanted to get to know me?"

"Of course."

"But what if I couldn't move my body an inch and I couldn't touch you or kiss you or make love to you and I couldn't feel anything? Would you still have fallen for me?"

"Nata . . ."

"Tell me the truth, Vladi. I won't be mad."

"How can I separate your body from your mind and your heart when I love it all?"

Of course she is unhappy with this answer. She doesn't say so, but her brows drop and she stares at the ground.

"You read too many books, Nata. You're always thinking the worst things."

"Maybe you don't read enough. That's why you're always complaining you're blocked."

"I read plenty," I lie. "If I'm blocked it's because I'm stuck on this maldito island."

"You would leave me if you had the chance. I know it."

Again, a look of sorrow that makes me want to splash her face with a bucket of water.

"You're the one about to be fifty thousand dollars richer. Maybe you're about to leave me."

I don't really believe this, but when Natasha starts the game of punishing me for no reason, I can't help but play along.

She smiles, feeling confident once again.

I wonder if it's because she's young that she behaves this way.
I wonder if ten years from now, she'll grow into a woman more
like Lily.

When we go back to Natasha's place, her mother has calmed, sitting on the sofa. "Come, children," she says when she sees us enter.
"Sit with me."

Natasha goes to her side, and I sit on a chair across from the two of
them. Natasha's mother sighs and tells us she has come to a decision.

"We will accept their money and move when they ask us to," she
says. "I will buy another apartment. Smaller. Perhaps further up in the
hills, in Nuevo Vedado or La Víbora. I won't spend more than fifteen
thousand on it. I have a plan for the rest."

"What plan, Mamá?"

"Ten thousand will get an instant visa to the United States," Natasha's mother says. "Twenty thousand will buy two."

"We're leaving?" Natasha asks her mother.

She shakes her head and points to Natasha and me.

"No. You and Vladi are."

•

It used to be that ten thousand dollars would buy you a spot on a
powerboat shuttling across the Florida Straits in the middle of the
night. Now ten thousand will cover a visa's full bribe to completion
at the US Interests Section. No lines, no endless delays of two or
three years and nonsensical denials; instant approval and processing
of paperwork. A ticket off this rock called Cuba into the sky and the
new unknown.

I explain this to my parents, who watch me over their dinner of
pork stew. I already ate at Lily's. That she feeds me is the main reason
my parents don't give me much grief about seeing her. But tonight
I only speak of Natasha and how her mother has offered me a way

out of this country on the condition that I marry her daughter. It's not enough for Nata to have a marido, even if I promise to be forever faithful. She says her daughter deserves an esposo, bound by law and paper.

Natasha thinks our getting married is the easiest part of all this. The difficult thing will be to leave her mother here alone.

"It's not how it used to be," her mother said. "You will be able to come back and visit as much as you want and still have the opportunities that La Yuma offers."

"But why don't you come with us?" Natasha asked her, but her mother insisted she's too old to start over.

Then she relented a bit and said, "When you and Vladi have children, I will join you over there and help you take care of them."

For my father, there is no question.

"Go, mijo! What are you waiting for? Another revolution? Go!"

My mother is not so easily convinced. It's from her that I've inherited my skepticism.

"Do you love Natasha?"

"Yes." Tonight I have no doubts.

"Do you love this country?"

"Yes," I say, though of this I am not so sure.

Later, I go back to Lily's and tell her everything. She knows about Natasha. She knows to be discreet. But sometimes in bed I make the mistake of telling Lily I love her and then I regret it even though it's true, for that moment. I don't want to make Lily feel bad. She gives me so much when at times it feels as if Natasha only takes from me.

When Lily and I are in bed, it's as if she cares only for my pleasure.

"Lily," I tell her, "you are an amazing woman. Your husband is a lucky man."

"What about your Natasha? Do you fuck her the way you fuck me?"

"She won't let me."

But Lily never asks if I love Natasha. Not even tonight.

"You know if you go over there to La Yuma, you will have to work very hard. My husband tells me all the time how much he has to struggle just to survive. Nothing is free. You have to pay for the roof over your head, every ounce of electricity and water you consume. Every time you flush your toilet. You have to pay for the air you breathe."

"I know what it is to work, Lily."

"You? You've never even had a government job. Do you know what I did before I had my daughter? I cleaned toilets at the Calixto García hospital. Do you know what happens in hospital bathrooms? The worst kind of waste you can imagine. I cleaned it all with my bare hands because most of the time we were short of gloves. Tell me, what work is it that *you* do?"

"I write."

"You haven't written five pages in the year I've known you."

"It takes some writers a year to write a perfect sentence."

"You can live on your invisible words here, Vladi. Not over there."

I think of Natasha. She once told me her first memory was of her sister dying. Natasha was three and her sister, Yulia, five. Their parents had taken them to a swimming pool near Marina Hemingway, and within hours Yulia was burning with fever, a raw wound blossoming around a small cut on her elbow. They thought the bacteria would only take her arm, but she died her first night in the hospital. They brought Natasha to say goodbye though she was already gone. She remembers the sight of her sister, hard, purple, and swollen. I told this to Lily once, and it is the only time I've seen coldness wash over her face, her voice hollow as she said, "Children die all the time, Vladi. It's nothing unusual."

•

My father had a girlfriend as a teenager, long before he met my mother, the daughter of a once wealthy family from Camagüey who owned property all over the island that was seized by the revolution except for one house on the edge of Miramar that the family was permitted to keep and live in. As it was forbidden to have American dollars, the girl's father hid the hundreds of thousands of bills he'd accumulated, lining all the paintings with money, stuffing stacks under floorboards, between walls, burying piles beneath rose beds in the garden.

There was so much money that he could not hide it all, and the man was so tormented by his fortune, terrified he would be discovered and imprisoned or executed, that one day he took all the dollars and made a pile of it behind the walls of the backyard, careful so nobody would see, and set it ablaze. There, the family watched as their fortune and inheritance burned, leaving nothing but scorched earth and the smell of smoke and ashes, which cleared with the afternoon rain.

"What is the lesson here?" my father asked his son when he finished the story.

I did not have an answer.

Was the lesson that one should not get attached to money or that one should not trust the government?

Was the lesson that if the man had held on to those dollars long enough, there would have been a time when it could have bought freedom for all of his descendants?

"Tell me the lesson, Papá." I wanted to know what I was supposed to learn.

"I don't know, Vladi. You're a smart boy. I was hoping you could tell me."

•

Sometimes in my notebook I write suicide notes. Not because I want to die but because I think it's an interesting exercise to see what sorts of things I have to say about my life, and also because I want to test myself, to see if I really have to write the last letter

of my existence, to whom would I address it: to my parents, to
Natasha, or to Lily.

*Dear Natasha, You make me fucking crazy. You still hide your
body from me when we are naked. You talk and talk and talk.
But then you go quiet and I love you more than ever and I want
to rip you open like the sofa so I can love every bit of your
bones. You are my conscience, and this is why I so often want to
escape you.*

*Dear Lily, I remember when you saw me on the sidewalk and
asked me to help bring your shopping bags to your apartment.
Within minutes you were sucking me off as if you'd been
waiting for me all your life. You make it hard to leave you. On
the street we are strangers, but in your home, you know me
best.*

*Dear Mamá y Papá. You raised me not to want what I don't
have. You didn't give me a sibling because it was impractical,
and this is why I hate practical things. In my corner of our
home I found solitude and have learned I never want to be alone,
but alone is the only way I know how to be.*

•

There are new barricades up around the Campoamor, so until it is dis-
mantled by road scavengers, Natasha and I can't get in. On my way to
see her, I ask one of the construction crew working on the Capitolio
what plans there are for the theater, restoration or demolition, but he
doesn't know.

"It's been rotting for over fifty years," he says. "For all we know, it
will rot for fifty more."

I stop by Abel's place. He's out of phone cards, so he can't refill
my minutes. We sit in his room, where he shows me on his com-

puter the piece he's working on for this month's contraband USB press, talking about how the government is displacing people yet again, not to make room for ministries and offices, like they say, but to sell entire buildings to foreign companies for luxury hotels and condominiums.

"You think that's what's really happening?" I ask.

"There are always money motives behind the official story," Abel says.

He's been telling me for a while about all the foreign investors and enterprises coming to the island, looking to get a claw in before anyone else; technology executives, car manufacturers, even the exiled rum heirs trying to get back in the Cuba-future tournament and compensated for what was taken from them so long ago.

"What is your family going to do with the money?"

"My parents are going to buy a place in Playa. They want to get away from the noise of the city. My sister is going to live with her boyfriend. I might find an apartment of my own around here if I can. What about Natasha and her mother? What will they do?"

"They don't know yet," I say, because Natasha's mother has sworn us to secrecy. She doesn't want others to get the same idea and ignite a situation where you have to pay a bribe just to pay another bribe.

When I go to her apartment, Natasha is waiting for me, the door wide open. She sits on the sofa, and I sit close to her, ease her horizontal so that we are two long bodies locked together by ankles and elbows.

Her mother has made the appointment for each of us. The first five hundred dollars went to getting us scheduled for the same day with the same employee.

But before that, another appointment. The filing of papers for a civil marriage. Natasha says it's not a real wedding. It's just a legal decision.

"So we won't really be married?"

"We will be, but not in the eyes of God."

"Since when do you believe in God?"

"Since we decided to get married. A civil wedding is bad luck. We need to have another wedding in a church. We can do it in Miami. With a party and everything."

"We won't have any friends to invite. We don't know anybody over there."

"Ay, Vladi," she says, and turns her body over so that we are nose to nose.

When we arrive in Florida, Natasha's mother's second cousin, whom she's never met, will meet us at the airport and let us live in a room he made out of the garage until we get organized and find our own place. Since I've known her, I've told Natasha I know how to speak a little English. When we get to the United States she will see I've been lying.

She says the first thing we will buy when we have enough money is a computer for me so I can transfer all my notebooks to a hard drive and finish my novel. A big American publisher will distribute it. It will tell the truth about *everything*, she says. I don't know where she gets these ideas, this certainty.

Before I came here to be with Natasha, I was with Lily. We were naked on her bed, the metal fan in the corner of the room blowing hard over our sweaty bodies.

"If I didn't have a husband, maybe we could be something, Vladi."

"Maybe."

"When it's time for you to leave, don't say goodbye."

"I won't."

We took a shower together before I left her, and sometimes I wonder how it is that if Natasha knows me as well as she thinks she does, she can't sense Lily on me, read on my face that I've made love all afternoon the way I read it on hers after we're together.

Natasha, I think. *Who are you? Who am I? Who are we really?*

But then it's as if she feels my distance, and it's Natasha who begins to strip me, pulling me on top of her, and I ease into her, support my arms on the wooden edges of the torn sofa where I fell in love with her, my eyes fixed on the black orb of the Capitolio cupola blocking the sunset just beyond the window, and next to it, the Campoamor, its clandestine residents and starving animals receding into a pond of gray and blue shadows.

GUAPA

You would never know by looking at me that I used to be more than double my current weight. The loss isn't enough to get me featured in a magazine or on a news program, but it was a lot for me, this small frame, pudge pockets I'd been carrying for decades, since I had no father and my mother thought the best compensation was food. I was one of those rotund babies who can barely move, who would topple over when placed atop a bed and need help sitting back up. I blamed my mother for overfeeding me, distorting my body practically from birth, but she was the first one to tell me I was predisposed by God for largeness and that I should not worry because what nature gives, art can fix. I was a teenager before I understood she meant surgery.

In the factory, everyone still calls me la gorda even though I'm now thin, my once-wide thighs narrowed to pegs. My ass went so flat with all the dieting and pills that I had to get it refilled with synthetic injections to recuperate lost volume. My breasts, which became nearly concave, were replaced with manufactured ones imported from France, and when I lie down, they hover above me as if saluting the sun. I haven't touched my face yet, but it's in next year's budget. Everyone thinks I fly home to Colombia for two weeks every year to spend time with my mother, but it's really for my surgeries. I'm still recovering from my fourth aggressive liposuction, which was more of a sculpting, to carve out my waist, the softness over my pelvis, so I can have a prettier vagina. Every summer, my friends from the factory go to Rockaway Beach but I always claim to be sick or busy. This summer they will see me in a bathing suit I bought on my last trip home. I tried it on the day after the operation over my compression garment, even though I was sore and swollen and blue everywhere that the needle had sucked and dug.

Edgar is the only one who never calls me gorda. He calls me guapa instead, just like he calls all the other ladies sweet names like hermosa, preciosa, linda, or bella. Lorena, who works on the packing line beside me, says guapa is the least desired of all the names Edgar gives to the women of the factory, but I don't mind. I see how he looks at me when he delivers the pallet of boxes to the end of my line so I can pack them full of tiny ceramic penguins or ballerinas, bottoms proudly stamped with MADE IN USA. I see him look my way as he drives his forklift along the corridor toward the warehouse. At lunch, he always finds me outside by Don Pepe's food truck and sometimes even pays for my croquetas. He doesn't know this is the only time I allow myself such decadence. In the mornings, I eat only fruit. In the evenings, only vegetables. On weekends, I eat almost nothing at all. I am so hungry, but it's the only way I can sustain this new body.

Sometimes he brings me mangoes he buys on the street near his home in Washington Heights. He takes the 172nd street guagua with the other Dominicans in the morning and back in the evening. I ride the guagua from Dover with some Colombians and a few Puerto Ricans. When I'm through paying for my surgeries I will buy a car, and this way I will be able to offer Edgar rides home.

He's fourteen years younger than I am but he told me once, as we stood in the parking lot smoking a cigarette together, that he likes older women. His first affair was with a young friend of his mother's who taught him to make love when he was fifteen. This was in Barahona, where his mother still lives in a house he paid for with his money from the factory. The first years in New York, he thought, just like we all do when we arrive, that he would eventually go back once he had something saved, but now he's been here long enough to know there is no returning—once you cross that ocean and those borders, they cross over you.

I know he's had relations with other women on our shift. There was Julissa, who works in Quality Control, young like him, and he might have loved her until one day they were no longer speaking and soon she was pregnant with Rolando from Dispatch's baby. They both work at a cargo company in Newark now, and Edgar moved on to Leidy and Prisca who are both old like me. But those relationships didn't last either. In those days, they were more attractive than I was, but I have made myself into something far superior now. My neck may still droop, but if I wear my hair down nobody can notice. I'm dotted with holes, I've got some indentations, and my breasts are lined with scars, but it's nothing that would catch your eye in bedroom lighting.

We kissed once. It was fast but forceful, out in the parking lot during one of our breaks, which we always take together. He'd stopped smoking by then, but he would still join me outside, even in winter, and on that afternoon, the bruised and moldy sky ready to break with rain and all the others already back inside, he pushed his lips against mine, our teeth clanked, our tongues slipped into each other's mouths, and then, like lightning, it was over, and he said something only young men say, something like *I wanted this*, or *I was waiting for this*, or maybe it was *You wanted this, guapa*. To tell you the truth, I can't remember.

•

My mother named me Indiana after what she said was the most beau-
tifully named state of North America. This was in Cali where all the
girls of my generation were named María or Ximena. My name, my
mother said, would be my destiny. She's still alive, in the house that
belonged to her mother and father. When I left I was twenty and my
mother took me up to the church of San Antonio on the hill facing
the three crosses shining over the valley, protecting the city from the
demon Buziraco. She said some people were born to stay and others
were born to leave. She was sure a better life waited for me on the
other side of the Americas. When I arrived, a friend of a friend met
me at the airport and took me to her house in Dover. It wasn't really
her house but one she shared with seventeen other people, mostly
Colombians like me, who didn't yet have social security numbers
or enough cash to pay rent anywhere else. We lived five or six to a
room, slept on floors or mattresses, if there was one available. I cried
through my first winter from the lack of sun, the cloak of snow, and
the wet chill that filled the house as we slept. But those people comforted me, fed me, dressed me.

The tears will pass, they said, and soon you won't even remember how
to cry. I don't know if this was true for them, or words they told themselves to endure the distance building between them and their own
countries and families, but I listened. And then it was as they said. In a
year, maybe three or five, I stopped crying and decided this was home.

The same woman who brought me to that house brought me to
the factory. She said the owner was a good man who hired Colombians without hesitation and who paid fair. They started me cleaning
bathrooms. I didn't mind. I cleaned offices and beauty salons back in
Cali, and I knew how to do things fast. Then they moved me to the cafeteria. I was to keep it clean, especially after the lunch rush, when the
men left their garbage all over the place. If I were better with computers, which is to say, if I had ever used one in my life, maybe they would
have moved me into one of the more administrative positions. But I
wasn't good for that. So they promoted me to packing boxes. I like the

rhythm of it, especially when the speakers overhead blast a song I like. Luckily Toño, the plant manager, is in charge of the radio station and likes salsa and merengue just like us. The classics. Grupo Niche and Joe Arroyo. Sometimes it feels like the whole factory is singing along with those songs we grew up dancing to with our cousins and our first loves. I had a first love, though you might never have guessed it since in those days I was at my absolute biggest and hardly left the house because everyone in the barrio called me la cerda. He was a neighbor. A boy who could be with almost any girl he wanted and still, he chose to come over to my house when my mother was out and be with me.

I told him I loved him and asked if he loved me, and he said yes, of course, otherwise he wouldn't sleep with me just like that. There has to be some kind of love there, he said. He told me I was a good girl and said I could even be beautiful with some effort. Not quite a reina de belleza but maybe pretty like one of the lesser-known telenovela actresses or bikini models like Natalia París, who was short like me.

"I know you have it in you, Indi," he said. "You just have to try."

He died in a motorcycle accident. The most wonderful thing was that his family donated his organs to science, and then we heard there was another man his age walking around with one of his kidneys, and another man somewhere who got his heart. I had dreams for a while that I would be so sick that I'd need a transplant and they would operate and give me a part of him. Maybe a lung, his spleen, his liver, or even his eyes and that way I could see the world and even myself as he did. I knew from an early age that I would never be able to have children due to a malformed uterus and one lonely ovary. But I thought if I found myself close enough to death, one of his organs could save me, and it would be better than giving birth to his child because he would be the one living in me.

•

I share an apartment with my friend Soraya, who works at a bakery on Blackwell Street. She has been trying to convince me to come work full-time with her. She says I won't have to do the hour-long commute to the factory every morning and night, but I wouldn't give it up for anything. I spend each ride sitting in the front row of the van, planning things I will say to Edgar during our breaks, during lunch, practicing the way I will smile at him when he brings the pallet with the empty cartons or takes my packed boxes away on his forklift. And when the guagua driver pulls into the parking lot and I see Edgar standing along the brick wall by the back entrance with some of the others, waiting for me—la gorda!—to descend, I tell myself and my mother in my mind, and even the demon Buziraco if he will listen, there is no other place I would rather be.

From the way I talk about him, you probably imagine a guy with movie star looks, some kind of prince, moneyed and polished. Edgar is all those things, or maybe none of those things. It doesn't really matter. I can tell you about his eyes and lashes and canela skin and broad shoulders that make clothes hang off him like drapery. I can tell you about the way he smiles, his front tooth angled outward, his sloped posture, the way he swallows half his syllables and makes fun of my singsong Spanish, and you would still not understand his beauty, his brilliance even though he can't write more than a few words much less read. I know this because he confessed it and yes, that's something that makes a man more appetizing to a woman, especially a woman like me: being made a man's confidant, his secret keeper.

No matter that Edgar is twenty-eight and I am forty-two. In the factory, with summer heat blowing through the vents like fire, where we stand in front of the rusted metal fans unashamed of the sweat dripping down our collarbones, dampening the seats of our jeans. In winter, the icy humidity of the Hudson penetrating the concrete and cinder block, when we work in our warmest coats, the fingertips of our gloves sliced off so we can still easily pack our boxes and load our pallets. Here, we are the same: two working bodies, and I think only of another kiss waiting for me in the parking lot, hot and wet and hungry just like the last. In the apartment I share with Soraya, carved out of the basement of a house owned by an Iraqi family, I dream of a life with Edgar, not in his country or in mine, but in this one; a life new for both of us.

•

Everyone is talking about the Christmas party. The boss booked an entire restaurant on Bergenline, with a dance floor and everything. Normally our Christmas parties are here in the factory, with food served on foil trays and all our dancing happens between the cafeteria tables. But this year business was good, productivity above average, and there were no lawsuits or union disputes, so we deserve to be rewarded. All the Dominicanas are planning to wear gowns normally reserved for weddings and quinceañeras, with salon hairdos and their best joyas de fantasía. The men will wear their funeral suits. The Colombianas and Puertoriqueñas don't want to look underdressed in comparison and many have bought new dresses or borrowed ones from friends. I have a dress I bought with some extra hours I worked at Soraya's bakery packing holiday cakes. It's royal blue with a cascade of beads along the chest and down the back. Satin that fits like skin. Secondhand but you would never know.

Soraya is twice divorced and thinks it's odd that I haven't been divorced even once as is normal for a woman my age. I didn't have to marry for papers. My green card came clean and easy, and everyone said I was so lucky but I thought it was the least God could do for me. I don't want you to think I've been celibate all these years in New Jersey. I've had plenty of lovers in my days as both a gorda and a flaca. I had a Syrian lover for a very long time, even in the first months that I knew Edgar. Perhaps I would still be with him, but he couldn't take the homesickness and returned to his country. Not even a war could keep him away.

Edgar worked in other factories in the area before he came to ours. The worst, he said, was a brewery in Queens where the boss locked them in from dawn to dusk. There were monthly raids, in which someone usually got carted off due to false papers.

"It's always sad when you see a compatriot taken away," he told me. I nodded.

He touched my hand. "We are the lucky ones."

This was back when I used to clean the cafeteria and Edgar would find me there sweeping and float around the tables while I worked. Sometimes Gilmer, Pinto, or one of the other guys would stick his head in and make a whistling sound or start singing a love song and we'd both roll our eyes, as if the idea of the two of us as sweethearts was beyond the possibilities of this world.

The summer of the blackout, when the factory went dark as outer space, Edgar found me by my packing line, took my elbow, and led me to one of the emergency doors—not the one everyone else was rushing toward, but another one, on the far side of the building where we found ourselves completely alone in a patch of parking lot, warmed by peach afternoon light.

"Why did you come looking for me?" I asked.

"Because you're my guapa," he said, and embraced me in the way of two lovers who have been together a very long time, resting our arms around each other's torsos with ease and familiarity. He held me close. I was still wearing the compression garment from one of my liposuctions and hoped the pressure of our bodies wouldn't make my wounds ooze through the bandages.

•

I gave up smoking a few months ago. It was my last vice to go after ice cream and chocolate bars. I was used to stopping temporarily in preparation for each of my surgeries, but I always took cigarettes back up because I found them to be great company in the solitude of my life in this country. I can tell you how poisonous and deadly they are, information you can get anywhere else, without denying that smoking brought Edgar and me together those first days. But now that we are both healthier people, and have both tasted each other's lips, we don't need them as excuses to come together.

Now, in the mornings, Edgar waits for me outside the factory with a cup of coffee from Don Pepe's truck. It's bitter and oversugared, but I drink it even as it singes my insides because it came from Edgar. He always arrives to work first, since his guagua only has to make that short trip over the George Washington Bridge. The Dover route is eternal, along the Christopher Columbus Highway where there is always traffic, but on most days we manage to arrive just before it's time to clock in.

Edgar greets me every day with a kiss on the cheek. He's not even shy about it. If you were to ask anyone on our shift who Edgar's girl is these days, they would tell you, without hesitation, it's la gorda. Maybe they would say they don't really know or understand what our story is, being that we live far apart and only see each other on weekdays, but those moments are loaded with promise, and if there is a romance brewing in this ancient building, it's not between one of the pregnant machine operators or one of the line mechanics with three or four novias. No, it's between Edgar and Indiana. What we have, anyone would tell you, is true.

•

On this morning, my ride arrives at the factory first. The workers who came on the St. Nicholas Avenue guagua say that right after they crossed the bridge, a tractor trailer turned over on the upper level and there you go, traffic like it's the end of the world. Edgar's van got stuck behind it.

A streak of springlike days has hit New Jersey. It's no longer frigid as a morgue. The grass in the lot next to the factory grounds has resurrected in a bright and fluffy green; even the birds and squirrels have emerged, hyper and shameless. A group of ladies gathered by the factory entrance brag to one another about their dresses for the party. I'll show them. They'll see la gorda dressed like Miss Universe, with hair extensions and fake lashes I've already bought at the beauty supply, all my surgery swelling down, my body starved and deflated and contoured to perfection. Mami was right. *What nature gives, art can fix.* On my next trip home, I'm going to bring my surgeon a gift to show my gratitude to him for my new life.

I ask Don Pepe for two coffees, one for me and one for Edgar. He lives with a cousin and his family on 167th Street. He's told me he sleeps on a sofa in the living room. He has the money for something better, at least for his own room somewhere, but he sends most of what he earns back to his mother. One day I asked if he wants to have his own family someday, and he shrugged.

"I'm not like most men. I don't care if I am never a father."

He doesn't spend weekends like some of the other factory guys, drinking, dancing, putiando all over the west side. Edgar prefers to stay in and watch television or play computer games with his cousin's kids. If the weather is nice he might go play soccer with friends at one of the fields nearby. If he's seeing a lady, maybe he will take her for walks in the park or to a party. From what I've told you about his other factory novias, you might think Edgar some kind of mujeriego, but it's just the opposite. No woman has been good enough for him, his pure heart.

One of the women who lived in my first residence in Dover, the house that turned over tenants like the Port Authority, has her own botánica in Paterson now, and when I'm feeling desperate, usually before a surgery, I pay her a visit for a little spiritual cleansing and white magic trabajo for good luck. She's a casual hechicera. Not like those brujas and magos who make you pay hundreds of dollars for all sorts of initiations and curse-breaking. This one is more about service. She just wants her community to be happy. I told her about Edgar, and she said she would take care of it for me, and I wouldn't even have to do something pathetic like slip drops of period blood into his coffee to make him love me. All I had to do, she said, was light a white seven-day candle and burn the petals of a single rose each night until they became ash. And then I was to collect that ash in a sachet of silk and bury it in the backyard. I had to wait until the Iraqis upstairs were sleeping in order to do this, because the wife is very protective of her flower beds.

Don Pepe hands me the coffees, and I return to the brick wall by the factory entrance. Everyone is waiting until the last second before the morning bell rings to go inside. There are no windows where we work. The factory is a long charcoal tube, like a subway platform, and in the winter, with overtime, we can spend the whole day in there without seeing the sun rise or set. My mother, the one who wanted me to come here so badly, often asks me why I stay. It's been twenty years, she says, and my life has not drastically improved since my arrival. Other immigrants do far better—start their own businesses, marry, have children who will be educated and able to provide for them in their old age. I have none of that.

"Maybe it's time you return home," she says. "You can take care of your mamita. We can be old ladies together."

I understand her impulse. I am her only child. But I tell her, "No, Mamá. It's not yet time."

•

The morning bell rings, and most of the parking lot crowd drifts into the building for work. The last thing you want is for Toño to see you're not yet at your station when the production lines kick in. You never know his mood. Sometimes he will let it go without writing you up, or, you might later hear your name called over the intercom system and find yourself sitting in Human Resources begging to keep your job. You might think this is just a factory, and why would anyone beg to keep working here, but the fact is there is a waiting list of people hoping to be employed. For every line worker, there is another handful of relatives or newly arrived friends who've heard about this place and are looking to get in. There are people who've worked here twenty, thirty years. Parents, children, even three generations of a family all on the same production line.

I want to wait for Edgar. I want to be the one to hand him his coffee when his guagua arrives, before he goes inside to work, so I hang around outside while the others disappear. My friend Rosa, who works the same line as me, sticks her head out the door. "You'd better get in soon, Indi. Toño's making rounds."

I tell her I'll be right in. Besides, Toño can't go hard when there's an entire guagua of workers late for their shift for reasons beyond their control. Toño thinks he's better than us because he has some kind of degree in who knows what.

"You could have Toño's job someday," I once told Edgar. "You're smarter than him. All he does is babysit us like we're in a daycare."

"You think so?"

"You're the smartest guy in this whole place," I said. I could tell it was what he needed to hear. Everyone needs positive affirmations. I heard a woman on TV say that once.

I hear the van's old engine before I see it tear into the lot. Rusty is driving. His only job in life is to deliver people over the bridge and back at the start and end of the factory's three shifts, and he's usually as careful as a surgeon. But today, no doubt with his passengers complaining they might have time deducted from their checks for being late, he rips across the pavement toward the back of the building, where I lean against the brick factory wall holding Edgar's coffee.

I search past the tinted windows for Edgar's face. I know he sees me. The van comes closer and closer, and I approach to meet it, but it doesn't stop; it keeps rolling and rushing as if delivering its passengers straight through to the other side of the wall, and I am pinned, the bumper pressing my thighs, the grill and hood, cracking my ribs against the brick. I feel nothing, only hear the crash, the skidding, and then screams.

•

My legs were severed. Well, they were still attached by something. Tendons or ligaments or fibers, I don't know for sure. Only that they were unusable. My pelvis, shattered. A few ribs too. My organs appear to be intact. They keep saying I am very lucky.

Many years ago, when Colombia played in the World Cup here in the United States, before the famous autogol that eliminated them and cost poor Andrés Escobar his life, the country was celebrating the national team's defeat of Romania. I'd watched the match at a cousin's house, and in the hours after, walked home alone wearing my yellow jersey, the streets packed with cars waving national flags from the windows, horns honking, joyful victory chants and already fireworks overhead. I was crossing a jammed intersection, inching between two cars stopped one behind the other at a red light, when I felt one car roll forward and push me against the one ahead. It was less than a second, this awareness that I would be stuck there, my legs cut as if by a blade, but I felt something lift me, carry me out of danger and place me on the sidewalk. I was shaken and told my mother the story when I got home. She had no doubt angels had saved me. Nobody else would have been able to lift a gorda like me like a bird carrying thread. It was a miracle if you believe in miracles. Or just an unexplained mystery if you don't. But it happened. I'm still here. All of this is to tell you that I'm not surprised I wasn't so lucky the second time. This time Buziraco got his way when he said, "Gorda, your legs now belong to me."

•

My friends from the factory brought me a card that everybody signed wishing me a quick recovery. *Recovery.* Such a funny word. As if my legs have only been misplaced and might still be found. I picture them walking around the factory, waiting for my return. *This is what you get for being late to work*, they will tell me when we are reunited. But no, they took those scraps of flesh and bone wherever they take detached body parts. I wonder, now that I have time to think about such things, whose job it is to pick up those human pieces, to discard them in the hospital trash.

Edgar signed the card near the bottom. He only wrote his first name, in letters of uneven sizing. I remember little about the crash.

They tell me I was on the ground for a long time, before the ambu-
lance and police came, before they assessed the mess of my body and
decided what to do with me. I bled so much they thought I would die.
But my system has always been good at clotting. I know this from all
my surgeries.

I remember Edgar kneeling on the concrete beside me. His face
close to mine. I don't think I was crying, just dazed from the shock,
heat shooting through my bones.

I remember asking what happened, and Edgar said, "Hold on,
Indi. You're going to be okay. Just keep talking to me."

I felt very sleepy then very cold, and I sensed the wall of people
standing nearby watching and crying. I heard the big boss's voice. I
heard the medical workers. Then I was no longer there.

They determined it was an accident. The break on Rusty's van
malfunctioned. It wasn't his fault, and there will be no criminal
charges. He may be able to sue the car manufacturer or the garage
where he had his last tune-up. I don't feel the need to blame. I know
these things happen. Bad fortune is as certain yet unpredictable as
the weather.

I lie in bed and feel my phantom limbs, kick them into the air,
practice the steps I was planning to try when Edgar asked me to dance
at the Christmas party. These were moves I'd rehearsed with Soraya
in our basement on many nights, the music turned low so the family
above wouldn't complain.

"He's going to fall in love if he hasn't already," Soraya told me.
This Soraya was full of hope for my future. Soraya today only looks
at me with mournful eyes.

"I knew you should have come to work with me at the bakery."

It's too late for such thoughts but I forgive her. I forgive everyone.

•

A guagua full of my friends from the factory comes to see me at the
hospital. Edgar is among them, but he hangs back. They've reduced

my pain medications, sewn my stumps with thick black socklike seams at what used to be my thighs. I keep them covered when guests come because I realize most people can't handle the sight of my nubs, and still, their eyes drift to the flatness under the white hospital sheet.

They take turns coming to my bedside and holding my hand.

"We love you, gorda," they say. "We miss you so much on the packing line."

The Christmas party has already passed but they have the kindness not to mention it to me. Their faces are sad, and I feel I must be the one to make them feel better.

"I'm not dead. They'll give me new legs, and I'll be back on the line soon. I know it."

When Edgar comes to my side, the others clear the room so we can be alone.

"Indiana. I don't know what to say."

He holds my hand, or rather, I hold his. He is the one more in need of comforting. I hear the others whispering in the hall. It's not their fault they can't gauge their own volume.

"It's such a tragedy," someone says. "All that work she did to her body, and now this."

My mother has already suggested this was some sort of punishment or retribution for the ways I've gone against nature to change my appearance. I was cheating God's design for me, she said, becoming vain, and I needed to be humbled.

My mind flashes with images of Edgar pushing me in my wheelchair, helping me stand on my new legs that actually make me taller, like a model or a beauty queen. I see us dancing together, me in my blue dress, Edgar shaved and glowing in a dark suit.

I tell Edgar a few lawyers have come to see me. They heard about my case and say I might be entitled to compensation. The factory's insurance company will surely want to settle because there should have been a safety rail or something protecting the entrance from incoming cars. One lawyer says I could get millions.

"We can take my new robot legs and travel the world," I tell Edgar. He smiles. *I* would call it a smile, not counting the tears in his eyes. "I have to go, Indi. They're all waiting for me. We have to get back over the bridge before rush hour. I'll come see you again on my own. I'll figure out which bus to take and come soon."

He kisses my forehead, and I'm embarrassed because I know I've got the hospital stink even though the nurses bathed me in bed this morning and helped me brush my hair nice so it covers my shoulders. I would hug him, but my pelvis is casted and I can't shift my weight.

•

Arrangements have already been made for my mother to take me back to Cali with her once the doctors decide my body can handle the journey. The only thing we know so far is that there is nobody to care for me here, to help me with all the necessary things, the ugly things, going to the bathroom, learning to walk. I would have to go live in a special residential facility. Years of therapy await. A psychiatrist told me nightmares will come when it settles in that half of me is missing. But I will adapt, the doctors say. All humans do.

They warn me not to get fat again because it will make it harder to walk on my new legs. Little did I know that by losing all that weight, I was getting myself into optimal condition for life as an amputee.

My mother tells me I should consider myself blessed. Not because I didn't die under the guagua but because I might get some money out of the whole endeavor. "Just think how all those people back home who've had their limbs blown to bits by land mines have no such luck. Maybe you'll make friends with some of them," she says. "There are support groups for people like that. I saw it on the news."

This is her first time in this country. She has seen only the airport, the hospital, and the basement where Soraya takes her to sleep each night in my bed pushed along the window near the good radiator. When she comes to the hospital to see me each morning, she proclaims, without fail, that she's almost grateful this accident happened because it's going to bring me home to Colombia with her.

She sits on a chair thumbing the pages of a magazine she bought in the gift shop downstairs. She says she doesn't understand how I endured so many grim winters or what kept me here year after year. It's not the future she hoped for me. So many people come to this country with much less and accomplish so much more than I have with my little factory job. Why, for such a life, she wonders, did I try so hard to be beautiful?

I don't argue or try to explain. I want to save my words for Edgar. Maybe he will come see me tomorrow or the day after. I want to think of a funny joke or story to tell him so that when he looks at me his first thought is not pity. But my mind is tired. The doctors warned I would feel this way for a while due to the trauma on my body, the loss of blood. My mother asks if I can hear her. *Indiana, Indiana,* over and over. But I only roll my head toward the window. Through the glass, there is only brick in place of sky.

LA RUTA

THE HEAT WAS MURDEROUS, BUT THAT MORNING, THE ENTIRE CA-
nine species of Havana seemed ready to copulate. I saw a dog huddled
against an archway on Paseo del Prado, penis protruding, red as an
American fire hydrant. For a moment, he stared at me as if requesting
mercy. In a shaded arcade farther down the avenue, a bitch in heat
stood, legs wide, her ass an open doorway. Three mutts of varying
sizes surrounded her, taking turns trying to climb onto her back as
she growled and showed her teeth, until the largest of the dogs settled
onto her spine, biting at the fat of her neck, and she cried, paralyzed.
I and a few other strangers paused under the balustrades to observe
the act, remembering a time when my mother would have covered
my young eyes with her hands and dragged me away with her quick
steps, but as hastily as it had started between the beasts, it was over.

I stopped on the median where the permuta crowds gather looking to make a home trade, to see about registering our place. It could
take years to find someone who wants to swap apartments; maybe
sooner if we were lucky and found a three- or four-way exchange. But

Florencia insisted nobody would want to move into a cavernous relic with tilted walls on a fourth floor in Centro Habana. *If it's not good for us anymore, why would it be good for someone else?*

The permuta market was a mess of shouts and tangles, brokers taking notes on who had what property in their possession and who wanted to move where. I tried to get in on the chaos, telling as many people as I could that I had a one-bedroom in decent condition to trade, with electricity and running water, but I could see I'd need a few hours for this endeavor, time I didn't have when the morning rush had already passed and I'd not even begun my work on la ruta.

I walked back to my taxi. It's never been mine, but I drive it all day, so I can't help but claim ownership over that Frankenstein; a 1950 Chevrolet shell with a 2009 Hyundai engine and Kia parts, painted matte black with plasticized seats until my cousin gets the money to replace them with real leather. It's his car, you see. Bought with a decade's salary from working in the machine rooms of oil rigs from Mexico to Brazil, Trinidad to Venezuela, ten months at a time. It was a dusty carcass when he purchased it from a junk collector in Boyeros. *You'll never save that piece of tin,* the guy warned my cousin even though he was used to the resurrection of every kind of condemned machinery. It took years of investment and mechanical experimentation by some of the most experienced machinists of Havana. I drove a delivery truck in those years, but my cousin told me to have faith. His almendrón would be ready one day—next year, he'd say, or maybe the year after—and he'd hire me to be a real cash-collecting taxi driver.

Now my cousin sits in his house in Nuevo Vedado all day, enjoying the air-conditioning he recently had installed, playing dominó with his neighbors, watching DVDs pirated through his Mexican connections and going to bars at night in search of a girlfriend. I drive his almendrón, up and down las rutas, along avenues from Marianao to Regla and Bejucal, giving my cousin his daily cut of thirty CUC, which I earn in seven or eight hours on the road. What I earn beyond that, I get to keep.

After I left the permuta crowd, I paid the parqueador his due cha-vitos for minding the car. He wanted to know how long and how much the restoration took—everybody wants to know what it cost to get our Frankie running, Cubans and tourists alike. I told him six or seven years, and ten thousand dollars. He let out a low whistle.

"For ten thousand dollars, you could have gotten yourself onto a yacht and off this island."

The bitch I saw earlier came waddling up the sidewalk, taking refuge in the space between me and the old man, leaning on my legs, until one of the male dogs, on the trail of her scent, discovered her, and again, she ran off with the mutt behind her.

"It's nature," the man said, with something that resembled nostal-gia. "If only life for the human animal could be so simple."

I heard a small voice behind us.

"Excuse me, chófe', are you heading on your way soon?"

She could have passed for a schoolgirl, but she wasn't in a uni-form, and later, when we came to know each other better, she would tell me she was twenty-six, though that day I wouldn't have aged her past eighteen. She wore a long, loose dress printed with flowers or swirls—I recall only that the dress set her apart, when all the other girls I took as passengers in my cab seemed to prefer the short and the tight.

"I'm heading up Reina right now," I told her.

"Will you take me?"

I motioned to the car door, and she let herself into the back seat, so that when I got behind the wheel she was just behind me and I could see no more of her in the rearview mirror than the black lacy edges of her hair.

It wasn't long before the car filled with passengers. There were arms out all over Prado, people waiting for an almendrón to pick them up and take them farther along the route. The girl sat in the back next to an older couple carrying a basket of flowers on their laps until they got off near the cemetery, and then a pair of students from the University of Havana climbed in, headphones in their ears, music so loud we could hear it over the newscaster's voice and the tick-tock of Radio Reloj. Beside me in the front seat, a sniffling woman, older than my mother would be if my mother were still alive, and a young girl in her care who stuck her hands out the window as if trying to catch the wind.

The girl behind me asked to be let off by the Sagrado Corazón church. I felt her fingertips graze my palm when she paid me for the ride. I wanted to tell her it was free, that I would drive her anywhere. I wanted to tell her how to reach me, give her my number, or at least tell her my name and where she could find me on the route in the mornings, but I felt foolish, because I'd barely registered her face beneath the dark halo that seemed to rise from her mane as I shifted to get a better view of her. She slammed the door shut behind her, and I cocked my head out the window to see as much of her now as I could, but she'd already disappeared into the crowd navigating the stretch of sidewalk outside the church, and though I saw the pale motif of her dress somewhere in the pedestrian tableau, the rest of her was gone.

•

A family of cats made their home on the tin overhang between our window and the building next door. The thin white father cat watched over the patchy mother cat as she lay limp, her three babies kneading and sucking on her tiny nipples. I once thought of capturing a kitten to bring inside for Florencia and me to care for since we don't have children, but she said cats were disgusting and would make her sneeze and cough even though she's not allergic. I could never argue. The apartment was in her name. We weren't married and she'd remind me often when we fought, threatening to throw me out, that not one millimeter of the space we'd shared for years belonged to me.

Rain fell that night, finally cooling the city. I sat by the window to feel the breeze, watching the cats that didn't seem to mind getting wet. Florencia had the television so loud you'd think her deaf, but it was because our set was competing with the TV next door. She was watching a Korean soap opera. She loved them. They were all tears and tragedy, not dreamy and romantic like the Mexican telenovelas about peasant girls marrying land barons, which Florencia said were hopelessly out of style. She was thumbing through a fashion magazine she'd rented from a lady who collects issues left in hotels by foreigners. Every few minutes she'd hold up a page for me to see, point to a dress or a pair of shoes on a skinny model and say, "Why don't you buy me something like that someday, Mago? You never buy me anything nice."

This was not true. I'd bought Florencia many nice things. I bought her the television she devoted most of her life to, and the new oven in the kitchen to make her life easier, even though she only complained that it still wasn't big enough for all the croquetas she had to make to fill her orders. Florencia was a psychologist, trained to cure insanity, or something like that. "Psychology should be a good business on this island," she'd say, "because everyone here is depressed." But she gave it up to peddle her mother's secret recipe for fried finger-size breaded pork logs, making hundreds a day to sell to shops around Centro Habana and La Habana Vieja. It was illegal work. Like everything around here. Selling contraband croquetas, sometimes even to government vendors. But Florencia took the risk for the handfuls of cash she'd collect each day, and sometimes, after she paid her assistant and her delivery boy, and covered costs for ingredients, she'd make up to fifteen dollars by sunset, more than she would make in a month listening to people's problems.

"I could do my hair like this," Florencia said, showing me a shiny page with a red-lipped girl on it, her dark tendrils piled high on her head.

"It looks like she's wearing a salad."

Florencia shook her head and turned back to her magazine.

"Estúpido," she muttered, loud enough for me to hear it but low enough for me to pretend I didn't.

I enjoyed the silence between us until it was time for bed. I left Florencia in the sala with her beloved television and pulled the sheet over me, hoping she wouldn't join me until I'd fallen asleep and that she'd leave me alone until I could sneak out before the first roosters of dawn woke her.

But I heard the TV switch off and Florencia's footsteps entered the bedroom, which wasn't really a bedroom but a space we'd forged out of the apartment with cinder blocks and vinyl sheeting.

"Your problem is you don't appreciate me, Mago," she said, even though my eyes were shut and I breathed heavy, as if already dreaming.

"I know you're not sleeping. Stop being such a fraud, country boy."

I'm not a country boy, but my parents were country people, from Ciego de Ávila, and Florencia loved to bring this up, calling me guajiro, mocking my manners, which she said were that of an old man, saying I wasn't hip like she was, that when I turned my back people laughed at me for dressing so conservatively, my hair grown to my ears and parted on the side, not shaved down or upswept into a gelled crest like every other guy around. *There goes Mago the Jehovah's Witness!* Me, with my country name—Margarito—even though she's the one who started calling me Mago, saying I had to be some kind of magician to somehow convince a city girl like her to be with me.

"I'm too tired to argue, Flor," I said, "and I don't even know what we're arguing about."

"Do you know how many men look at me when I walk down the street?" She was kneeling on the bed next to me, needling my back with her fingers so I'd face her.

"I have no idea."

"Dozens. Maybe hundreds."

"Lucky you."

"I'm blond, Mago. Do you know how many women would kill to have my hair color? Do you know how many men would beg me to have their baby just so it will come out rubiesito like me?"

"Please let me sleep, Flor."

She shook my shoulder so I had no choice but to finally turn to her. I saw the outline of her small body, backlit by the moon, glowing in her white underwear, her face obscured by darkness so I couldn't see the hard lines of her jaw, the cut of her cheeks, those light eyes she flashed to strangers as if they were diamonds, still poking my arm like a child, scratching my skin with her broken nails.

"Do you know that yesterday a man stopped me on the street because he thought I was American? American, Mago! How many Cuban girls do you know who can pass for a Yuma?"

"Not very many."

"Liar. You don't know *any*. Only me. And do you know what this man said to me when I told him my name?"

"Why did you tell him your name?"

"He said I had the same name as one of Italy's greatest cities. He said it was one of the most beautiful places in all of Europe, full of history and majesty. He said it suited me."

"Did you tell him it was just your grandmother's name?"

"You're not smarter than me, Mago. Don't try to make me feel dumb when you're the one who didn't go to school past thirteen."

"I'm not trying to make you feel anything, Flor. I'm tired. I've been driving all day. My back aches. Please, just let me rest."

"You think you're special because you drive your cousin's almendrón and you make more money than I do. I'm the special one, Mago. Look at me with my glorious hair that God gave me. I'm like an angel in this dark hell. You don't deserve me. Everybody tells me so. That's what people think when they see us on the street together. Your worst crime is you don't even know it."

•

I picked up three girls going east on Neptuno, just as I dropped off a lady on the corner of Infanta. They took up the back seat while the front seat beside me remained empty. It was barely afternoon, but the girls were dressed as if going to a party, one in a glittery skirt, the other in pants that looked like your fingers might stick to the fabric, and the other, in the sort of yellow dress one might otherwise wear for Ochún. The girl in the skirt said, "Remember always to smile. Even if you don't know what they're saying, even if you think they've just insulted you. Smile, smile, smile."

"And touch his hand or his arm any chance you have. They love that," the one in the pants said.

The girl in yellow received these instructions with nods while the other girls continued.

"You can sleep there, but get out before any housekeeping lady sees you or you'll have to tip her to keep quiet."

"Look sad when you say goodbye. It makes them feel important."

"Don't ask if he's married. Don't ask if he has children. Don't ask anything except what work he does and then look very impressed and say you never met anyone as successful as him."

The girl in yellow laughed, and the other two scolded her.

"You're getting the benefit of our experience, Claudi. Don't be an ingrate. And make sure you leave with plans to see each other again."

The girls didn't notice my eyes on them through the mirror. I'm good at stealing glances when passengers think I'm just watching for cars. These girls were young. Maybe eighteen or nineteen. With makeup and jewelry, it was hard to tell. The fact that they had makeup and jewelry at all told me they were at least old enough to have found a way, for a while now, to pay for it.

They asked if I could keep driving along the bend down Prado so they wouldn't have to walk so far in their heels. They would tip me extra, they said. And when other people tried to flag down my almendrón on the way, the girls commanded me from the back seat to ignore them, and said they would tip me more to keep the ride private too.

They got off just before the park, and I hopped out and pretended to check the engine so I could buy some time and see where they went. I saw them step onto a terrace outside one of the hotels on the avenida and there, three men stood up from a café table to meet them with kisses, their pale hands lingering along the girls' backs.

I thought of Flor. Once, during one of her annual depressions, she told me it was her bad fortune to have been born in Cuba a pearl-skinned rubia who struggled to keep every kilo on her gaunt frame, unable to make a dollar on her body since foreigners came to the island looking for the voluptuous dark-skinned women of the travel brochures and Tropicana posters.

I'd never seen the area so packed with tourists, not even in the winter when all the Russians and Canadians come to Havana, and we were only in July, each afternoon flushed by rain. I stood around a few minutes before a policeman had a chance to chase me off since only government taxis are allowed to park in front of hotels, hoping to catch the eye of an adventurous foreigner, the kind who have figured out how much cheaper it is to travel in an almendrón than a tourist cab or even a Coco-Taxi.

"Chófe'" a voice said, and I knew it instantly, though it had been months since I'd seen her, heard her, saw her faded dress slip away in the crowds.

"Are you working?" she asked.

This time I got a good look at her, waiting for her to recognize me. Her dark hair swept to one side, curls that had been brushed out with care, stray strands sticking to the sweat at the base of her neck. She wore another long dress, sleeveless with buttons up the front. Navy blue, a color too heavy for such a hot day, and patches of perspiration marked the creases beneath her ribs.

"Yes, I'm working," I told her. "I was just taking a break. The car is all yours. Where would you like to go?"

"I was hoping you were planning on doing the Boyeros ruta. I'm going to El Rincón."

She studied me. I was certain then that she knew my face too, perhaps that, though she couldn't connect me to the exact moment

we'd met a month or two ago at almost this very spot on Prado, she
sensed the familiarity between us as much as I did.

"To San Lázaro?"

She nodded.

"I'll take you," I said. "I always have a reason to go that way."

•

She sat in the front seat, leaning on the door, taking in the smell of the
ocean as we passed the Malecón. I played with the radio dial, but every
station only played news and I decided music was better so I put in a
disc, but when the first reggaetón song came on, she turned to me with
a gentle frown and asked if I minded not listening to anything at all.

I wondered if she'd noticed how I'd driven past people with their
hands out along the ruta, wanting to go in our direction. I wondered
if she could tell that I'd wanted to ride in the car alone with her, even
though we hardly spoke, even though someone called her on her mobile phone and she told that person she loved them.

Flor called me too. I ignored it like I usually do, so that I don't
have to waste unnecessary phone minutes, and she knows to call a
second time only when it's urgent. This time she didn't call twice, so
I wasn't worried. I don't miss Flor all day like I did in the early days
of our love. It was almost ten years ago, when I was thirty-five and
she, thirty. We both left other people to be together. We thought we'd
found the source of eternal joy in each other. We thought we would
never want anybody else.

We passed through the sloping roads of Santiago de las Vegas, and
I turned onto the tapered path to El Rincón. A lone horse chewed
on a pile of cut sugarcane. A cluster of barefoot children rolled co-
conuts around as if they were marbles. People stood in doorways of
clapboard houses selling purple flowers, tobacco, beans, and rum, for
pilgrims to bring as offerings to San Lázaro, or the orisha, Babalú Ayé.
There were beggars gathered at the gates outside the church property,
as usual, among vendors of prayer cards and rosaries.

"You can leave me here," the girl said.

"I can wait for you. It will be hard for you to find a ride back to the city so late in the day."

"You don't mind?"

"I have someone to visit here. We'll meet out front when you're ready to go."

Some of the beggars came right to the car and followed us until we were past the gates, asking for limosnas, and the girl and I each divided our chavitos among them. A man with no legs tried to sell us purple candles for the santos. The girl bought two.

She went into the church, but I walked ahead toward the hospital behind it. I hadn't been in a few months. Flor says my visiting doesn't really make a difference. My father no longer understands the passing of time. Sunrises and sunsets mean nothing. He doesn't know that one day ends and another begins. He doesn't see himself or me grow older, and doesn't remember that his wife died decades ago. For him there is only this perennial hour—the haze of dawn or twilight—every face before him, a benevolent stranger. The doctors, the nuns, the other patients. Even the face of his own son.

•

They told me my mother died of pneumonia. I remember when she became sick, a strong woman suddenly frail, her complexion grayed until she dissolved into her bedsheets because she refused to go to a hospital, and they took her away. My father raised me alone in that apartment near Ciudad de la Libertad. He was a policeman until the spots became so bad, pink and white blotches on his brown skin, bumps rising, flesh peeling away, sores opening, denting so far in at places I was certain I saw bone. He didn't believe the first doctor who told him it was leprosy. *There are no lepers left in Cuba! It was eradicated by the revolution, along with the other evils.* But the doctors said that wasn't true, ask any dermatologist. Even though lepers were no longer forced into isolation, they preferred to remain hidden at places like the lazaretto of

El Rincón among those who suffered similar conditions, away from the stares, superstitions of castigos de Dios, and the cruelties of the pueblo. I told him I would care for him at home just like we had cared for my mother, but my father said he wanted me to be free of him. As I think of it now, those were the months during which my father first started to lose his words, the names for certain objects just out of his grasp, the names of people we knew blanching from memory.

My father had been at the hospital for thirty years. Since I was fifteen and an uncle came to live with me after my father left. When I returned home after completing my military service, the uncle told me he'd convinced my father to sign the property over to his name, so I had to find another place to live. I complained to my father about it, but he'd already slipped into a limbo of time and reason even though he wasn't yet fifty, and gave me the puzzled, empty stare I would learn to accept in place of what had once been an expressive face, eyes that could hide nothing. So I left the matter alone and found a friend who let me sleep on his azotea.

The guards at the hospital gate stopped me, telling me the santuario is *that* way, pointing to the church.

"I've come to see someone at the hospital."

They raised their brows, surely because those who live in the lazaretto rarely get visitors, but they let me through.

I found my father in the room he shared with five other men. He sat in a wheelchair by the window, his once strong hands knotted by arthritis, his chest recessed, his back rounded and neck shortened like a hutia. He sat beside an old woman even smaller than he was, in her own wheelchair, wearing a white nightgown that showed the outlines of what was left of her breasts, the few white hairs on her head combed flat against her scalp. A nurse told me the woman came from her room to visit my father in his every day.

"Viejo," I said, kneeling before him. "I'm your son. Margarito. You are Octavio, my father."

He stared at me with curiosity, reaching out his shaky fingers to touch my cheek.

"I know you," he said, and for that second, it might have been true, but his gaze quickly left me and turned toward his companion, who had a similar stare, as if she were seeing through my father into another place, one in which everything was not yet forgotten.

The other residents were quiet as they sat and took in the space of the white concrete room, the soothing view of the garden and a tree with chirping birds. There was noise down the corridor; conversations between nurses and nuns, the murmur of a radio.

I held his hand for a few minutes, rough and hard and cold in my palms. He'd lost feeling in his hands long ago, and though a blanket covered his knees, I saw his ankles had vaulted inward. He watched me with a vacant look, and I worried I was making him uncomfortable, forcing him into a moment of tenderness with me.

I told my father I would come see him again soon. I said it aloud and again in my mind, unsure of which way he would be more likely to hear me. I told him I would come next time with Flor, who never knew my father as the elegant uniformed officer he was, the one the neighborhood was proud to call their own. She'd come with me only twice to see him. She said it depressed her to be among the lepers and senile even if they weren't really contagious. Nobody wants to be reminded of sickness and death, she said, even if she was a psychologist and supposedly trained to deal with people in distress. I thought she would want to at least be a comfort to me, but when I asked her to accompany me to see my father the next time, she said she would rather I go alone.

•

There were dogs roaming the church property. These were no longer strays, adopted by the groundskeepers, given names like Milagros and Santiago. Even the mutt one of the janitors found as a puppy, tucked beside the plastic baby Jesus in the Christmas crèche, was named Noel. There were seven or eight of them, but the groundskeepers kept them confined to a fenced garden when the church was crowded. One of them told me it was because humans couldn't be trusted. They were capable of harm even if they came here to pray. One man had spent hours in the shrine only to walk down the church steps, find a small mutt napping on the pavement, and pick it up by its neck until he nearly crushed the animal's throat. One of the groundskeepers saved the dog, asking the man why he would do such a thing, but he had no answer. The groundskeepers said it was their duty to watch over the dogs since dogs had been the only friends of San Lázaro, after all, walking with the man of the parable, licking his wounds as society shunned him.

The feast day of San Lázaro was a dangerous day for the dogs, I was told; the santuario packed with the devoted, carrying out promises, dragging themselves on their knees, raw from the pebbled road, pulling large boulders with ropes tied to their legs or shoulders. When my mother lay dying, my father made a promise to San Lázaro that he would join the pilgrims, making the procession to El Rincón on his knees on December 17 like the other faithful and penitents, and wear purple for all his remaining days, if only the saint would cure his wife, but his prayer went unanswered. Maybe when my father became ill, I should have tried making a similar promise to save him. I never did.

But when I came to El Rincón, I still liked to go into the small room they made to house the ex-votos; glass cases holding proof of prayers answered. Golden trophies belonging to Olympic athletes, baseball players; knitted baby shoes in gratitude of miracle births, children brought back from the clutches of death; photographs of families reunited after long separations, and medals from veterans of wars in Angola, Bolivia, Ethiopia, and Grenada.

I pressed my face close to the glass to read a letter in fading ink written by a mother describing her child's recovery from alcoholism, touched by the mother's gesture of writing a letter to a saint most people say never existed. I noticed I was no longer alone in the room of the ex-votos. The girl I'd brought in the taxi was also taking in the tokens of thanks. We moved about the glass cases quietly. I was aware of her, just as she was aware of me. But I didn't want to speak, taking us both out of the spell of faith in that small room, as if we might each absorb a trace.

When we got on our way back to the city, the girl pulled a small notebook out of her purse and wrote something down.

"This is my three hundredth church," she said.

"What?"

"I keep track."

"You've been to three hundred churches?"

"Well, there aren't that many in Havana, so most of them I've repeated several times. But I've been in a church each day for three hundred days in a row. Today was a special day. That's why I wanted to come all the way out here."

"Why do you go through all that trouble?"

She paused, as if unsure now that she'd started a real conversation between us, but continued. "I've been asking the santos for something almost all my life, but they never heard me. Somebody told me I had to make a big promise, show them how serious I am about repaying the favor even before it's granted. I promised I would visit a church every single day for a year until they hear me."

"You don't get tired of going to churches?"

"Of course I do. But that's the point of the promise. All those virgins and saints have to know how bad you want it."

"What is it you asked for?"

She was quiet, and my instinct was to apologize for being so blunt, but then she turned to me, and I saw her face directly before mine for the first time. Her lips were thin and toasted by the heat, and I wanted to run my fingers over them just to see what she might do.

"I have an aunt in San Diego. That's in the United States. Since I was born, my parents have begged her to claim me as family and bring me to live with her, but she said she didn't want the responsibility of looking after a young girl. Now I'm twenty-six. On this island, practically an old woman. But I'm married, so I've been asking my aunt now that I have a husband and we will be responsible for each other, if she will finally file the papers to bring us over so we can try for a better life over there. She says she's thinking about it. That's the reason for the prayer and promises. To help her decide."

That she should want to leave this island, even though I still didn't know her name, somehow felt personally hurtful. Even more than the fact that she was married.

"I've never prayed for anything," was all I said.

"You should try it sometime."

Raindrops began to fall on the windshield. A few moments later, we were driving under the thickest clouds in the storm, streaks of water sliding in through the windows, which we rolled up, and the air in the car grew warmer between the girl and me.

We edged down Vía Blanca and the girl asked me to leave her near Calle Aguacate. She had to go to work, she said.

"What is it you do?"

"I'm a typist for a poet. He says he's blind, but I would swear I see him watching me as I sit in front of him. I think he just likes to hear his voice but not the actual writing of words. I'm good with my fingers though. My mother taught me how to play piano when I was a child. I could play with my eyes closed. She thought I could be a professional, but then some Spaniards offered her money for the piano, so she sold it."

"And your husband?"

"He doesn't play the piano."

"No, I mean, what does he do?"

"He's works in tourism. Sometimes they let him be a guide to foreign groups, which is the best, because he makes tips. But sometimes they just keep him in the office."

"You don't wear a ring," I said, immediately fearing I'd made her uncomfortable.

She looked down at her hand and rubbed the finger where a band should be.

"We're saving money for other things first."

I thought of Flor, who said the only reason to marry was if you were going to get something out of it like a visa or property. Beyond that, there was no point. "Love, sex, children, family," she'd say, "you don't need marriage for those."

I'd wanted to marry her for a time. I was traditional. Perhaps I still am. But Flor laughed at my desire to make her a bride as if I were trying to con her just to get my name on the apartment deed.

When we came to the poet's address, the girl paid me, and though it wasn't nearly enough for what I would have charged anyone else for the long ride out to El Rincón, I told her I wouldn't take her money.

"Why not? It's only fair."

I shook my head and waved my hand so she couldn't drop any bills into my palm as she was trying to do.

"You did me a favor. Because of you, today I saw my father. He's at the hospital there."

She smiled and put the money back into her purse.

"Thank you."

"I'll take you to your churches. I'll meet you where I picked you up today, every morning at nine, and I'll take you to a different church so you can make good on your promise until you get your prayer answered."

She seemed uncertain as she studied me and finally said, in a voice that was lower and slower than the one I'd previously heard from her, "I'll let you take me. But only because my mother says you should never stop someone from trying to do something kind."

•

I woke up before the roosters even though it would be hours before I saw the girl. Flor stirred beside me and rolled onto her side to watch me dress for the day, her face tranquil, eyes still swollen with sleep.

"You don't kiss me anymore," she said, as I slipped my belt through the loops of my pants.

"What are you talking about? I kissed you yesterday when I got home. You didn't notice because you were busy watching the Koreans."

"You used to kiss me in the morning. When you woke up. When you thought I was still asleep. You don't do that anymore."

I leaned over to kiss her, but she turned her face from me.

"Not like that. It's too late. I'm awake. The moment is gone."

"When did you become such a romantic?"

"When I realized there was no romance left."

I put my shirt on and noticed a button was still missing even though I'd asked Flor to sew it for me days ago. I took it off again to see if she'd notice the reason, but she didn't. I reached for another shirt, a blue-and-white-striped one that once belonged to my cousin, who said he bought it in Lima.

"Flor," I said. "Why have we never tried to leave this island?"

"We're too old to go anywhere."

"But before. Why didn't we ever try?"

"Neither of us has anybody anywhere who can claim us."

"But there are other ways."

"I tried. Before I knew you." She was referring to the time she almost married a Mexican but the guy married another girl whose family was willing to pay more to send her off with him.

"Why did you stop trying?"

"I realized life is hard and miserable no matter where you live."

"You're miserable?"

She shrugged. "Things could be better. They could also be worse."

She got out of bed and walked toward the kitchen in her underwear. I tried to think back to a time when Flor was ever modest with me but couldn't think of one. She'd been the one to pursue me when I was with another woman. She'd found out I worked at a shipping facility in Jaimanitas and came there in a borrowed car and told me she was tired of her boyfriend and wanted to be with me with enough confidence for us both.

I heard her turn on the oven and pull out baking sheets and bowls for the morning shift. She spent hours alone in the apartment with her twenty-year-old assistant. It only occurred to me then that Flor's lack of modesty might not be reserved only for me. I walked over and met her by the sink.

"Give me some money, Mago. I've got to send Josué out to buy lard today."

"I'm short this week. Don't you have any?"

"I don't get paid until Saturday. Why are you short?"

"Yesterday was slow. I made only enough to pay my cousin."

"How could it be slow? It wasn't a holiday."

I didn't want to tell her about the girl or my trip to El Rincón.

"Just one of those days," I said, going back to the bedroom and reaching into the cigar box we'd bolted into a slat beneath the bed and took out some bills from our savings. I went back and handed them to Flor, who inhaled as if they were roses.

I said goodbye and kissed her cheek just as she said, "One day I'm going to leave you for a rich man. I may be too old to find a good-looking young one, but I can still catch a rich foreign viejo looking for a girl to take care of him until he dies. What do you think of that?"

"A fine plan, mi amor."

"You'll miss me when I go. Your life will be empty, but I'll write you letters from my new house and send you photos."

"How kind of you."

"And when he dies, I'll come back to Cuba and buy a big house so we can live in it together. And we'll never have to think of this rotting cave again."

"You'll be a hero."

"Yes, Mago. I know."

•

The girl wanted to go up to La Víbora, to the church of the Pasionistas. She was wearing the same dress as the first time I saw her, and the sight filled me with unreasonable hope, as if she'd worn it only for me. I'd gone to Prado early to try to get a word in with the permuta crowd again, remind everyone that I still had an apartment to trade, but there was no interest. I found her waiting by the almendrón, holding a newspaper over her face to block the sun, and despite the small patch of shade across her cheeks, I saw she'd gone through the trouble of putting gloss on her lips.

We were quiet for most of the drive into the hills, but I entertained myself by pretending the girl and I were on a date. I smiled at the picture I created of us as a couple, driving out of the city to enjoy a picnic in Parque Lenin, or on our way to Varadero or Playa Girón for a day at the beach. I thought myself the luckiest man in the world to have this pretty, gentle young woman at my side. The way she loved me, I imagined, was full of sweetness, her thin pianist hands grazing my neck with her fingertips whenever we embraced. She leaned against the window and watched the dusty city panorama blur past us, the dreamy girl who writes for the poet but doesn't care even to listen to his words.

I looked over at her, slouching in the seat inches from me, close enough for me to touch either her arm or her thigh, for her to hear me whisper that I hoped her prayer was never answered so that she'd never leave me on this island without her.

I parked in front of the church while she went in.

"Are you sure you don't want to join me?" she asked.

"No, you go ahead. I've got to mind the car."

She disappeared between the open doors and into the darkness of the church.

I stood by, taking in the downward slope of the hill, Havana pooling at its base, specks of white among blue, a shred of sea behind it. Here in La Víbora, wind curled though the green parks, among the shanties, and brushed against my face as I closed my eyes and pretended it was the girl reaching for me.

She returned to me a few minutes later looking somehow refreshed and wrote down the date and name of the church in her little notebook as we started on our way back down to Centro Habana. I drove her to the poet's home, and once again, she tried to pay me, but I refused her money.

"Don't try to pay me again," I said.

She seemed taken aback my firmness.

"You're the only person I've ever known willing to do something for free."

I wanted to tell her it wasn't free when she gave me a peace unlike any other, a respite from the crowds that normally fill my taxi, a private liberty in which I can play in our shared silence at an imagined intimacy, a life that will never be.

.

September mornings are dark until nearly seven. I pulled the car out of the garage and passed a guy walking a muzzled dog forced to drag a tire that had been tied by a rope to its neck. The man walked briskly and the dog, though muscled and wide, struggled with the weight of the goma as it twisted and rolled to its side. The dog tried to stop, but the man kicked it in the rear to keep it moving.

I rolled the car slowly as I passed the man and lowered the window.

"Why don't you give the dog a break? You can see it's tired."

"This is a fighting dog, asere. He's not allowed to get tired."

"There are police on the next block. They'll fine you if they see you."

"I'll take my chances."

The dog rested on its back legs as I distracted the man, the tire falling flat.

"You're torturing the poor animal."

I could see the man growing impatient with my delaying him.

"What do you know about animals? You drive an almendrón."

"I know what I'm looking at here isn't right."

"Nothing about this island is right. What about the tire I've got tied to *my* neck? Do you see anyone stopping to help me?"

He kicked the dog again, and they both started walking, the dog's neck dipping under the weight of the tire, the man tugging it up with his hands on the dog's scruff. I couldn't watch anymore and started the car in the direction of Galeano to start my ruta, to make as much as I could before it was time to pick up the girl.

I'd been driving her for nearly two months, even on Sundays, my only day off, and telling Flor I'd been hired by an old friend of my mother's to run errands. Together, the girl and I visited dozens of churches, some, multiple times. Each morning, she appeared from the archways on Prado and we'd ride in an easy silence that she only interrupted to remark on the heat, to say the forecast predicted early rain, and when I'd drop her afterward at the doors of the poet, she would sometimes touch the top of my hand softly as she thanked me.

Flor only noticed that my daily earnings had thinned. I tried to compensate by starting my route earlier in the morning or finishing later at night, but it didn't make up for the prime morning hours I offered to the girl to help her make her promise.

That morning, when the girl found me waiting for her by the corner, she settled into the car in the way I'd memorized and tried to conjure for the rest of the day after she'd gone to her job and I picked up other passengers who sat in her place. Her shoulders against the upholstery. Her knees leaned toward me.

"I have something to tell you," she said. "Today is the last day I'll need you to drive me. I've fulfilled my promise."

"Your year is over? Already?"

She nodded.

"What happens now? Did your aunt file the papers to bring you over?"

"Not yet."

"Then why stop? You can start another year. Keep going until you get your wish."

She shook her head. "No. I've given up, chófe'. I won't do another day."

She wanted to go to the cathedral, since it was the first church she'd visited when she'd started her year of promises. I parked the car and walked with her to the edge of the plaza. I wanted to see her walk up the steps. She was in another of her long dresses, which, when I once complimented her, she told me she'd sewn herself; another hobby she'd picked up to make use of her restless fingers until they found another piano.

When she came out a few minutes later, her face serene and satisfied, we walked together back to the almendrón. A mother cat lay next to a shopkeeper's door, two kittens nursing on her. The girl stopped to watch and the shopkeeper stuck her head out to tell us the mother cat belonged to her but we could take one of the kittens if we wanted.

The girl bent over to get a closer look at the cats, swirls of orange and black on white.

"You should take one," I said.

"I don't want to love anything on this island. It will make it harder to leave."

•

I wondered if she noticed how slowly I drove when it was time to take her to see the poet, if she could tell that I did not want the morning to end because we'd run out of churches and days together.

When we arrived, I told her that if she should ever want to start a new year of promises, I would wait for her at the same spot on the same street at the same time every morning.

"You don't have to do that. I told you, it's finished."

"If you show up, fine. If you don't, that's okay too. I'll be there. It's not out of the way for me. It's on my ruta."

She smiled and touched my hand, the way she'd started doing since she'd stopped trying to give me money.

"Thank you, chófe'."

I never told her my name, and she never told me hers, though once, when I left her to her work with the poet, I heard a woman call hello to her from down the street before she stepped through the door. The woman called her Margarita.

•

Flor found us a permuta, and she did it without my help, as she emphasized, when we went to see the apartment together that night. It wasn't too far from our current home, on the edges of Barrio Chino, larger, though there were an extra two flights of stairs to climb, which made it an even trade.

"I don't want to move," I told Flor when we got home and were supposed to be thinking it over. "This place isn't so bad. And that place isn't much better."

"This apartment is mine to trade and mine to keep, Mago. I'm the one who makes the decision."

"I don't have to go with you."

I didn't mean it to sound like a threat, but that's how Flor took it. She stared at me as she settled into her favorite chair to watch television.

"That's true. You don't have to come with me. But we both know you have nowhere else to go."

•

I woke before the roosters. Or maybe I never really slept. I was waiting for the hour in which I could rise without arousing suspicion, dressing to start my ruta and make my way to the corner where I hoped the girl would find me even if for just one more day of her promise. Flor didn't wake, though she had to be up soon to start her morning croqueta dispatch. I leaned over to kiss her goodbye, so she couldn't bring up charges against me later, but when I came closer, instead of brushing my lips against her face, I pressed my fingers lightly into her cheek.

I was through the first hour of my route, driving passengers on their morning commutes, when Flor began calling. I ignored it at first, but she called again and again until I picked up, her voice panicked because Josué hadn't arrived for work and if she didn't make her day's deliveries, she would start losing orders.

"You need to come home and help me, Mago. I need you to make those deliveries for me."

It was nearly nine, when I was due at my stop of Prado, though there was no guarantee the girl would be there to meet me. I wanted to wait for her, even if it took hours, for a chance at the nourishment she'd given my days. But Flor was crying like I'd never heard her, or like I'd only heard her when money was involved, so when I unloaded the last of my passengers, instead of heading to Prado, I turned in the direction of our apartment to help Flor.

She'd meet me on the corner of Infanta, she said, to save time. As I approached, I saw Flor standing with three trays piled against her chest. She saw my taxi coming and stepped closer to the curb. I slowed the car but couldn't make myself stop. I kept driving and heard her shout my name several times, but I was already headed in the direction of the Malecón, watching Flor shrink in the rearview mirror. The phone started to ring, and I answered to her howls that I'd driven right past her.

"I didn't see you," I said. "I'll come back around now."

But I was already driving along the seawall, the waves spiking over the Malecón, covering the avenue in liquid sheen. Flor's calls didn't cease until I turned the phone off, parking the car at our usual corner on Prado, waiting for my favorite face to emerge from the shadows of the archways. I knew she would come. I knew she, too, had found some small sense of refuge in the space of the almendrón that she would find difficult to surrender. I waited, because I knew that even though she'd said she'd fulfilled her year of promises and had given her prayer legs of its own on which to stand, because she was a girl bold enough to have faith in the unseen, to know that there is no end to a promise, she would come to the corner to find me.

RAMIRO

RAMIRO WOULD TELL YOU HIMSELF HE WAS JUST ANOTHER SLUM KID from El Cartucho. He lived in a one-room apartment with his mother and another family of seven who let them take up a corner. They'd come from Pereira with Ramiro's father when Ramiro was just beginning to walk, but his father got stabbed beneath his ribs while shining shoes in front of the Palacio de Nariño and Ramiro and his mom had to find their own way. He'll tell you his story like he was some kind of miracle, not getting into basuco like every other kid in the sector. He was business-minded, he said. Even before Los Neros tapped him, he was hunting in dumpsters all over the zona for good garbage to bring back to the recyclers in El Cartucho; tins and shoestrings, or maybe he'd get lucky and find a whole rubber tire or a pair of shoes they could put back together to sell or trade.

Most of the people in the barrio were lost in a high or busy with a hustle, but Ramiro said living in El Cartucho wasn't so bad. People looked after their own and did a good job keeping everyone else out, throwing junk at outsiders who wandered in or just warning them they had five minutes to disappear or the people of El Cartucho would do it for them. Police never patrolled there and didn't even bother coming if called. At most, they'd show their faces in El Cartucho for a few minutes—acto de presencia—but leave quick before anyone had a chance to ask for their help. It wasn't unusual to see a dead body or two on his walk home, Ramiro told me, and I never questioned whether any of what he said was true. Vagabonds with old dogs at their sides, shriveled by the Andean wind, basuqueros killed by their last hit, or someone sunken to the pavement by bullets. It was like the war of the angels in there, he said, with no shortage of weapons. People used to joke El Cartucho was where the paramilitaries came for their guns. Any fool could buy or rent a pistol or a machine gun. Same for bazookas or grenades. You'd never know it by how miserably its inhabitants lived, Ramiro said, but El Cartucho was a real money factory. This was a long time ago.

It was Renata, one of the girls he grew up with in the apartment, girls he felt so close to he called them his sisters, who introduced Ramiro to Los Neros. She made some cash padding her baby's stroller with drugs or money, whatever Los Neros needed to get out of El Cartucho into a car waiting along the Avenida Caracas. Ramiro was just twelve at the time. He didn't want to be one of those kids carrying knapsacks of dealers' merchandise because those kids got regularly jumped and killed by lesser pandilleros in competing gangs. He wanted a more secure position so Los Neros made him a messenger. All he had to do was relay coded phrases from one gang member to another on opposite ends of El Cartucho, and they'd keep him flush with pocket money and bonuses like a nylon parka or new jeans. He did this for years until they promoted him to collector, and then Ramiro's job was to go around warning debts needed to be paid or Zaco, the rarely seen head of Los Neros, would be very unhappy.

On the news, politicians called El Cartucho a national disgrace, a dangerous and filthy boiling point just steps behind the presidential palace that needed to be victoriously extinguished like they'd finally done when they filled Escobar's body with bullets. When it got flattened into the park of El Tercer Milenio, most of Bogotá thought that would be the end of El Cartucho. The inhabitants, already desplazados, would just melt into the population, go back to the villages and valleys they came from, or, what the public really wanted, would disappear altogether. But the entire community just moved a few blocks south and, like the seven-headed dragon whipping stars from the sky with its tail, waiting to devour children, El Bronx was risen, becoming everything El Cartucho was and so much more.

That's where I met Ramiro for the first time. Though I never knew his name. I noticed the way he watched me standing behind my father, who was begging Ramiro's boss for a discount on perico. My father found the only way he could stop drinking was by replacing it with something else. He wasn't dumb enough—or *poor* enough, he'd say—to start on basuco like some degenerado de la calle. Cocaine was less grimy, he told himself—of the land even if it was cut with petrol and bleach. I was thirteen. Ramiro, seventeen. I wouldn't have remembered him all those years later, but he remembered me, said I had the same face now that I had then, unchanged, like I've been both a little girl and a grown woman all my life. I would have thought I was special, but Ramiro told me Los Neros were the ones who trained him how never to forget a face, even those of children because they are often the most vicious and vengeful.

It's in the eyes and the brows, he told me. Una mirada revela más que una huella dactilar.

A look reveals more than a fingerprint.

•

Ramiro was Padre Andrade's assistant, meaning whatever the priest asked, Ramiro had to do. It was a condition of his release. He'd gotten exempt from doing prison time again because some social worker recommended him for a service program, and Padre Andrade agreed to take him on in his church. Padre Andrade was notoriously compassionate, not like the other priests in San Ignacio's parish or serving in other churches in the area who really didn't want to get their hands dirty with the people. He told us he'd started as a monk but soon felt called to serve beyond monastery walls. He never had a bad thing to say. Not even after he got robbed at knifepoint in his own church.

I ended up at San Ignacio's after I'd been thrown out of another school for not showing up enough, and my father, having now replaced all his vices with religion, convinced the nuns to put me to work at San Ignacio's or he'd have no choice but to send me to a facility for bad girls like he'd been threatening for years, or worse, tell my mother how mala I was so that she'd never bring me up to Los Estados to join her like she'd always promised. But the only work I ever found myself doing at the church was cleaning alongside Ramiro.

"If you wanted me to be somebody's maid you could at least let me get paid for it," I told my father. But he insisted this work was to be an offering to God. Some kind of cleansing of the soul.

I spent my days mopping the cold marble church floors, dusting pews around the homeless who came to sleep on them. Ramiro vacuumed the rectory and offices, washing and ironing Padre Andrade's and the other priests' vestments. When he wasn't housekeeping, Ramiro got to sit at the front desk and answer phone calls, booking baptisms and funerals, taking down the names of the newly dead.

He was short and skinny, the way of just about every kid from El Cartucho, undernourished, raised on motorcycle exhaust and industrial fumes. He had small eyes that disappeared when he smiled, twisted teeth and black hair that sprouted into spikes when he took too long to shave it down. I wasn't tall but still taller than him, which meant he had to tilt his chin up to talk to me in a way that didn't make him seem diminutive, and when I looked down, I often notice he'd pushed himself up to his toes.

The first time we were left alone together in the rectory he asked me how I got to look so healthy, and how a comemierda like my papi managed to raise a daughter with such pretty white teeth.

"Don't call my father comemierda, malparido."

He grinned, apologizing, said he meant it as a compliment. It wasn't just the quality of my teeth that impressed him, which he insisted could only come from a childhood of regular milk-drinking, but that I had straight legs, knees faced front, not at all angled inward; the sort of build and stature only a parent with money can buy.

I didn't want to tell him, because my father told me it was our family secret, the money came from my mother who'd stayed in the United States after my father was deported. After my birth in a place called Virginia, she'd sent me back to Bogotá with a friend who left me with my mother's mother until she died and my father convinced my mother to let him have me until she returned to Colombia or was ready to bring me north. It was supposed to be a matter of a year or two, but every Christmas she'd say it wasn't yet time. She never failed to send the money though. She kept us living in a nice enough apartment and kept us fed when my father took long breaks from working as a chauffeur for rich people on account of his drinking.

"Don't ever tell anyone you're a gringuita," my father warned. "They'll attach themselves to you."

Instead, I'd be still as death when Ramiro would take a piece of my hair and rub it between his fingertips as if it were made of sugar, inhaling deep. He liked the smell of my shampoo, he said. *Expensive.* He'd finger my earrings. Tiny gold hoops sent to me from my mother for my quinces, telling me I looked good in gold but not as good as I could look in emeralds. And my shoes. Short leather boots my father had bought for me at El Andino because, even if he was mad about some trouble I'd gotten myself into, and even if he wore the same suit to work almost every day, he liked for me to have nice things. Ramiro looked down at my feet, shook his head, said nothing, yet I felt embarrassed. But then, one day when we were both helping at one of Padre Andrade's Sunday lunches for the poor, Ramiro, serving heaps of frijoles onto the plates of dozens who came to eat, let a big spoonful slip out of his grasp and onto my shoes. He didn't even say he was sorry.

•

Every evening around six, when the equatorial night drove the city into complete darkness, I took the TransMilenio home while Ramiro ate dinner with Padre Andrade and the other priests, then went to sleep in a small room they'd made for him behind the kitchen. For the first six months, he wasn't allowed to leave the church property, but then Padre Andrade started taking Ramiro with him when he'd go to hospitals to anoint the sick and give last rights. I think he wanted Ramiro to get a more human picture of those who were ready to die. Ramiro was never accused of killing anyone, and he'd deny it if you were to ask, saying sicarrio jobs are for kids—the expendables with no parents and no brains—but it wasn't out of the realm of reason to think he might have taken on some killing vueltas. Even I knew when you were in with Los Neros, you did what you were told. But Ramiro insisted it required wisdom to stay alive in his business. Half the kids he grew up with in that apartment in El Cartucho were dead now and when talking about them, he'd huff his nostrils and mention whatever dumb thing they'd done to deserve it.

"Just like the church has its rules to obey," he said, "El Bronx has its own commandments too. We all have to pay for our sins."

Sometimes he'd talk about the day my father took me with him to buy drugs, which had made a big impression on Ramiro. He remembered my father's look of desperation. He was a guy who still had a good face, not sunken and contorted like the other junkies drifting like zombies through the barrio. Ramiro and his boss could tell my father was a guy on the verge, who could still avoid the trap of total addiction, not yet like those other men, far more distinguished, former professionals, educated, even upper-class men who somehow ended up sleeping next to piles of waste, talking to themselves, begging for pesos to get their basuco to make the time pass easier.

What a lowlife, Ramiro had thought, *bringing a child to a place full of degenerados and pecueca, when he could just buy his little bag of coke from any dealer in El Centro.*

"Your father doesn't deserve you," Ramiro told me one afternoon in the rectory. "If I were him, I would guard you with my life. A daughter should be cherished, not used for sympathy to get a better deal on drugs like that band of beggars who sit on the sidewalks of La Zona Rosa with doped-up sleeping babies in their laps."

"Your papi looked down on us," Ramiro added after a moment. "But I remember thinking he was the real piece of scum."

Many years later I'd regret that as Ramiro went on insulting my father that day, I did nothing to stop him.

•

After one morning on a hospital visit with Padre Andrade, Ramiro came back to the church looking shaken in a way I'd never noticed in him before. We didn't have the habit of asking after each other. He'd eye me like I was someone's silly pet he had to tolerate, and I'd just listen to whatever he wanted to talk about—mainly how he'd rather be in prison where at least he could watch TV, smoke cigarettes, and talk shit, than here in a church living like a Franciscan and ironing the underwear of old priests.

He sat at the front counter of the rectory. Madre Naty had gone to the chapel for a few hours of Adoration of the Blessed Sacrament, so Ramiro was in charge of the phone and was supposed to help me assemble hundreds of pamphlets offering help to unwed pregnant girls.

"You should have seen this vieja," he told me while I stapled the papers together and he watched. "Padre Andrade's putting the oils on her and she looks like she's already mostly dead. Then she opens her eyes, sees me standing by the door, and screeches loud as a fucking parrot, '¡Mi hijo! ¡Mi hijo!' She waves for me to come over, and Padre tells her, 'No, señora, that's not your son, that's my friend Ramiro,' but she keeps crying, 'My son has come home to me! My son!' And just when I start walking over to her, in less than a breath, in not one second, she's gone, like nothing, like we're all going to be one day. Nada. *Gone*."

The phone rang, but he didn't pick up and gave me a stare so I wouldn't either. When it stopped, he took the phone in hand, dialed some numbers, and then I heard him greet his mother and I could make out the high hum of her voice coming from the other end. She never came to visit him at the church. I never knew why. But he could call her as much as he wanted. He told me he'd saved enough money over the years to support her living in an apartment with other older ladies who had no families.

"When I get out of here I'm going to buy a house for her and me," he said, as if the world were full of such possibilities. "You can come live there too if you want. If you want to get away from your father."

"No, thanks."

"What are you going to do when you get out of here, Chana?"

"I'm going to go be with my mother in New York," I said quick, without thinking.

He laughed. "Sure you are."

"It's true," I said again, in reflex, since I don't like to be contradicted.

He smiled.

"Okay. But when you go, don't forget to take me with you."

•

We'd both been at San Ignacio's about nine months when the guys started showing up to see Ramiro. It wasn't so obvious at first. I'd notice one or two of them in the church, not looking like they came there to pray or to sleep, but like they were waiting for someone, which wasn't so unusual either, since a church in between Masses is a great place to conduct a shady negocio. But these guys stood out to me. Then they started coming into the rectory, and I heard one of them, while I was on my knees organizing the file cabinets, ask Rosalia, the volunteer who was on the desk that day, if there was a guy who worked around here by the name of Ramiro.

"He's out with Padre Andrade," she said. "Would you like to leave a message?"

"Tell him Juancho was here. And that I'll be back."

"Are you a friend?" Rosalia asked, because all of us had been warned Ramiro wasn't allowed any contact with his old crew. His visits had to be approved.

"I'm his cousin."

I wasn't there when Ramiro got the note that he'd had a visitor. But I was there when Juancho came a second time. Ramiro was in the sacristy, cleaning the chalice, which took more than an hour given it was enormous and plated in gold and had to be polished with extra care since it held the body of Christ. Padre Andrade normally did it himself. He didn't even trust other priests with that chore, but for some reason, he trusted Ramiro.

"He's busy working," I told Juancho, who was small like Ramiro and kept his hands in the pockets of his leather jacket, looking all around as if he were afraid of someone touching him.

"Go get him for me."

There was no one else around, and something about Juancho made me reluctant to tell him no. I told myself no harm could come of telling Ramiro he had an unannounced visitor just this once. Besides, Padre Andrade was always making exceptions for him.

I went down the hall that connected the rectory to the church, the sacristy in between, and stood by the door because seeing all the relics normally used in Masses like simple objects in a storage space made me uneasy. Ramiro was surprised to see me there. Even more surprised when I said there was a guy named Juancho waiting to see him. The chalice was in his hands, so I knew he was still supposed to be in a state of reverence and shouldn't speak. He nodded at me, and I slipped back out, catching Juancho fingering the pregnancy pamphlets stacked in racks in the rectory, since we'd finally finished putting them together.

When Ramiro came out, he and his friend greeted each other with an elaborate handshake.

"Parcero," Juancho began, "I only came to tell you the dog has started barking again. The veterinarian says he's almost cured. We can start taking him for walks like we used to."

"Oh, really," said Ramiro. "That's good to hear."

"We just need to find the right medicine now. So he can keep getting better."

Ramiro nodded. "I'll see if I can think of something that will help him."

They shook hands again and Juancho then extended his palm toward me, but I was too slow to react and he seemed to take it as an insult and brusquely slipped it back in his pocket as he turned away to leave.

•

My mother didn't know I was working at the church. She thought I was still in school, and when she called on Sundays, her only day off from cleaning houses, she'd always ask how my studies were going.

"Wonderful," I'd lie.

And my father would help, lying too, "She's the top of her class." He'd trained me from the time I learned to speak to tell my mother how much I loved my papito and never wanted to leave him. I had no memory of knowing her, but she still spoke to me like I was her baby, telling me her plan was for me to join her in the United States and I'd learn English and go to a real American high school one day.

In the early years, it was true, I had been a good student. But around fourteen I started to change, sneaking out of the schoolyard and into the cars of the boys I'd met at the bowling alley, who'd wait for me outside, take me back to their apartments up in the hills, to fincas out in the savanna, guys who ran favors for men with money, who taught me to drink, to smoke, to take off my clothes, how not to feel anything. But they didn't need to teach me to lie. That, I learned at home.

Over the phone, my father and I gave our best performances.

I was all achievement. A dream of a child. It was to keep her money coming in those monthly chunks. It was wrong, I know. But my loyalty was to my father because, even if she was my mother, she was still a stranger, a woman my father resented because, when he got deported, rather than wait for him to find his way back to her, she divorced him. She had a boyfriend she lived with now, and sometimes that made my father jealous, even though he'd brought several different women to live with us over the years, though none had stayed too long, always fed up with his drinking, his depressions and crying and moaning through the night, and his blame on the US government for forcing him back to this place to start over.

I was out looking for my father one night after I returned home from the church and didn't find him where he usually was, waiting for me to cook him dinner so he could start his evening routine of television and a half dozen beers. That didn't bother me. It just relaxed him and didn't send him into a frenzy like aguardiente and whiskey did. Those benders were less frequent but I sensed this night, with its thick fog and wet wind, was one of those in which I'd have to go hunt for him. I started at the bar on the corner where the owner had the good sense to cut him off when he became too unruly, calling me to come for him. But my father wasn't there. I went to two more of his usual spots, but still, no sign of him. I was close to giving up, on the edges of San Bernardo, ready to head home and just wait it out because he'd have to return anyway, for money, for food, for a shower, for sleep, when I saw a familiar face across the avenue.

There was Ramiro, free as a dog out on the street.

He didn't see me. His attention was fixed on the two guys he was with. He stepped under a streetlight long enough for me to be sure it was him. Plus, I recognized his jacket, black with long white stripes down the sleeves, and his shoes, a battered pair of loafers; Padre Andrade said no sneakers in the church because their soles squeaked against the marble.

My father didn't come home that night. When I was already on my way out to the church the next morning, I found him sleeping in the hall outside our door. A neighbor had left a prayer card to the Virgin of Chiquinquirá on his shoulder. I shook him awake and helped him inside, then to his bed. I called his boss to say my father wouldn't be in today because he was home with a flu. My father watched me through one eye as I lied for him.

"Good girl," he said, then fell back asleep.

•

"Why don't you have a baby?" Ramiro asked me. "A girl your age should at least be thinking about it by now."

"I'm only sixteen," I said. Plus, one of my father's girlfriends, Zoraida, had taught me how to count my days as soon as I got my first period.

We were folding more pregnancy pamphlets. These were advertising a home where girls could go live while they were waiting to give birth and for a while afterward, where they could take classes in sewing, cooking, and computers.

"Sixteen is old enough," he said. "You should see the things I was doing by sixteen."

"You don't have any kids though."

"Who said I don't?"

"You never said you did."

"My sister Claudia—she's not my real sister, you know—she's been saying her son is mine for years. I doubt it though. I heard parents can recognize their baby by smell, and to me he smells like any other kid."

We could hear Padre Andrade in his office talking to some parishioner about her marriage problems, whether or not this lady could forgive her husband's affair. It was easy to eavesdrop, since Padre Andrade's office had a frosted glass door. Padre was insisting she at least try, since we're supposed to be all about forgiveness as children of God, and Ramiro looked to me, whispered my name, and waited until he had my full attention to say, "I'll give you a baby, Chana. We can make one, you and me."

I stared down at the papers in my hands.

"Don't be embarrassed," he said.

"I'm not embarrassed. I just think it's a stupid thing for you to say."

"It's not so stupid. I like you. Most guys can't stand the mothers of their children."

I kept to my folding and stapling.

"Are you afraid of me now because I said that?"

"No."

"You should be. At least a little afraid. You don't know who I used to be before I got here. You only know what I told you. And I only told you the easy stuff so you won't think I'm a monster."

He came closer to me. I was leaning on the counter, and he leaned beside me so our hips were almost touching, and I felt his breath flow upward against my chin and over my lips.

"I'm not afraid of you."

He watched me, maybe to see if I'd move away, stir under his closeness.

"Good," he said finally, and stepped back to his end of the counter. "I like that."

•

Sometimes, when he was at his drunkest, my father would say my mother didn't want for me to be born. He was the one who insisted on my birth. They slept in a car in those days and only washed in bus or gas station bathrooms. My mother said they could barely feed themselves and a third mouth would leave them to starve. When my mother sent me away, she wouldn't let my father have me. She said a borracho like him would be dangerous around a baby. She forbid him from coming by my grandmother's house to see me, but Abue relented every time he showed up at the door and let him in.

I remember long before she became ill, before the headaches, before the fainting spells that left her in bed for most of the day, before her body started to shrink and I held myself against her in her bed; once, after my father had sat with us for dinner at her table and promised me he'd take me to a carnival that weekend, we watched him descend the narrow stairs from my grandmother's apartment to the street, where he'd left his flimsy motorbike, and my grandmother said solemnly, "Your father is not a good man, Chanita. It's not his fault." I never doubted her.

When she became sick, it was my father who came most often to visit her. We thought she had a passing illness. Even the doctors said she would recover. She had been strong all her life. Nobody thought she would die.

She and my mother had made no plans for my care, so my father took over.

If I mentioned my grandmother at all to my father, he would say, "You were only three when she died. It's impossible that you can remember her at all."

"But I *do* remember."

I'd describe her apartment, the market where she worked a stand next to a spice vendor who made sweet teas for me to keep warm within the damp warehouse walls.

"Those aren't memories," my father would say. "Those are stories I've told you."

I remember, I'd insist, if only to convince myself.

•

It was Padre Virgilio who discovered the chalice was missing. It was a Tuesday morning. During preparations for the eight o'clock Mass, he'd gone to the sacristy and noticed it was gone. They'd used a spare steel one that was nowhere near as beautiful as the golden chalice that had been gifted to the church by some rich family years earlier. It was worth something, though Padre Virgilio wouldn't say how much when the police came to make the report and investigate the robbery.

Padre Andrade was traveling in La Guajira. Every year he made the trip with other priests to visit rural communities and churches that were little more than a few benches arranged in the sand. There was no way to get in touch with him.

Padre Virgilio sat Ramiro and me down in his office to ask what we knew of the chalice's disappearance. I'd never even seen the thing up close, I told him. And I never saw anyone besides the priests, the alter servers, the nuns, or Ramiro set foot in the sacristy.

Padre Virgilio turned his attention to Ramiro.

"I don't know what happened to it, but I assure you, I will do all I can to find out," Ramiro said. He told us he'd spent so much time caring for the chalice and cleaning it and felt a true divine presence every time he touched it. His voice became stilted, and he paused to catch his breath.

Padre Virgilio seemed moved by Ramiro's words. There was no thread of doubt in that room, even if the police were encouraging suspicion since one of the crimes Ramiro had been charged with before turning up at San Ignacio's was grand theft.

My father had his own theories.

At home, he'd made progress. Hardly drinking, attending more of San Ignacio's nightly meetings for alcoholics.

While I prepared our dinner one night, weeks after the robbery had turned up no leads of any kind, my father said, "I bet you it was one of those little nuns. How easy for a monjita to commit a robbery when you've got a criminal from the basurero living there for everyone to suspect first."

"You don't think it was Ramiro?"

"I don't think he's stupid enough to take the chalice. He'd do better stealing from the poor box."

Back at work, the only thing Ramiro ever said to me about the missing chalice was that whoever took it must have really needed it because it's no small thing to smuggle something that large and shiny out of the church and into the city.

"We may know the miracle without ever knowing the saint," he said, so certain of his words that I believed him.

•

By the time Padre Andrade came back, people had started to accept the chalice was gone forever, and Ramiro even had the idea to start up a special collection in order buy a new one. Padre Andrade said God was with us whether we had a beautiful chalice or a humble one, like the people he'd been with up in La Guajira who used cups carved out of wood to consecrate the body and blood of Christ.

But people around the parish still whispered, turning suspicions from one of the volunteers to Ramiro, or even to me, wondering who'd been the real thief.

•

The recyclers of El Bronx turned over the chalice some months later. A boy, probably a messenger-in-training, had brought it to them, they said, telling them his patrón wanted a good price for it since he knew they could break it apart and use both its metal and its gold. But the recyclers considered themselves faithful believers, and they knew that somewhere there was a church missing this chalice, took it out of El Bronx hidden in a banana crate and brought it to the nearest police station.

It wasn't long before they located the original kid who brought it in and pulled in another pandillero who started talking, revealing the trail to Los Neros, saying the chalice was sourced from none other than Ramiro, who still had debts to pay as a consequence of his arrest.

The police came for Ramiro on a Thursday when he and I shared the work of cleaning all the silver plates used for distributing Communion. The police didn't say much as they took him away. Padre Andrade was in confessions, so he didn't hear a word of it until he came back to the rectory, a startled expression on his face when Madre Naty told him Ramiro had been arrested and taken away.

"They know he did it," she said. "There are witnesses."

But Padre Andrade only shook his head. He went into his office, shut the door, and from the other side, there was no sound. Through the frosted glass of his doorframe, I could make out the shadows of his body, see him support himself on the edge of his desk, and lower himself to his knees to pray.

•

I wasn't surprised they'd found Ramiro to be the one. I'd always gotten the feeling, when I saw Padre Andrade leading him around, an arm around his back as if he were his long-lost son, that Ramiro was uneasy in this holy space. The rectory felt quiet and empty without him. I missed doing my mopping, my sweeping of the church aisles with him near me, but I knew it would eventually come to this. Just because they'd made a place for Ramiro in the church didn't mean he belonged there. He would find a way to ruin it, I was sure; it was a quality I recognized from watching my own father.

What I wasn't prepared for was the fact that Padre Andrade, after prayers and reflection, had gone to the police station and told them there had been a mistake. Ramiro couldn't possibly have stolen the chalice. And when they'd asked why not, Padre Andrade said Ramiro could not have stolen the chalice because it was Padre Andrade himself who had entrusted it to him to watch while he was away in La Guajira. He'd personally asked Ramiro to take it for a professional polishing so that it would look more lustrous in time for the winter fiestas.

"But, Padre," the police said, "You know Ramiro is not supposed to leave the church grounds as part of the agreement for his sentence."

"Yes. That part is my fault. I'm the one who sent him out. The one you should punish in this case is me."

Padre Andrade insisted Ramiro had been robbed. One of his old associates had seen him and jumped him. Ramiro, out of loyalty and shame, had remained quiet about the assault.

"Ramiro is innocent here. If you need to blame someone, blame me."

They asked Ramiro if this was true, and Ramiro looked to Padre Andrade, who gently blinked his eyes.

"It's true. Padre Andrade trusted me."

All this is what Ramiro told me later, when he returned to the church, because once again, the police released him to Padre Andrade's care and supervision.

But something changed in Ramiro the day he saw Padre Andrade lie for him. I noticed it the moment he walked through the rectory doors, more ruminative than as if he'd seen yet another person waiting to die as Padre Andrade gave them their last rites.

Everyone came out to witness his return to San Ignacio's. The other priests shook his hands because they could tell that's what Padre Andrade wanted them to do, even if their eyes still held bitterness for his betrayal. The nuns also welcomed him back, stiffly, and the volunteers stood on the edges of the rectory, looking even more skeptical of him than before.

I only waved at him. But when we were alone together later, cleaning out the wax residue in front of the statue of the Virgin and Child to make room for yet more candlelit prayers, Ramiro said to me, "It's going to be different now."

"What is?"

"I'm never going to leave here again."

I thought he meant they'd be keeping even more of an eye on him now, or that maybe it was easier to just stay on the church grounds and avoid bad company.

"But everyone knows you're here. They found you once, they can find you again."

"They might come looking but they won't find Ramiro. I'm someone else now. You're going to leave here one day, but I never will."

I didn't say anything because it seemed like he was just trying out the words for the first time, and I wanted to see if there was anything else behind them.

"You know what I like about the church, Chana? They'll take in anybody. Poor, homeless, shamed, desperate, addicts, criminals. Society's worst, and most sinful. People who've used up all their chances. Even screwups like you and me. In those ways, the church has got a lot in common with El Bronx and El Cartucho."

•

For a few more months, the days went on just as they had before the chalice was taken. Ramiro and me in our rhythm of work, until Madre Naty told my father she thought I'd graduated from my penance and I could stay to work there if I wanted, but maybe now I was ready for something else. She could see I'd learned about commitment and responsibility. She would write a letter so the school would let me back in, and they did, though I'd lost a full year. If I did extra assignments, they'd help me so I wouldn't fall further behind. This made my father happy, and it made it easier to lie to my mother when she called and asked how school was going, at least for a while, until I started skipping classes again to go off with the boys and my father finally made good on his promise to send me to a place for problem girls that was more like a prison.

But before I knew of his plan, before two thick men showed up at our door and my father watched as they forced me to pack a bag and pulled me by the arms out of our home, down the stairs, into a van waiting on the curb while I cried for my father to give me one more chance to be good; before that afternoon, we were at Mass together one last time, at San Ignacio's, where I didn't mind accompanying my father because I could tune out the gospel and watch Ramiro in his new role as altar server, looking almost righteous in his white robe, the wooden cross Padre Andrade had brought him back from La Gua-jira hanging from his neck. He'd grown his hair so that it fell into a neat side part and with new peace in his eyes, he somehow seemed younger to me than ever before.

With the choir voices vibrating against the stone pillars and the marble floor we'd cleaned so carefully together so many times, I'd recall our days in the rectory, the way he used to look at me, the way I would try not to look back. I'd study him there in his seat at the end of the altar until he sensed my stare, turned his head, and spotted me within the first pews beside my father and among the old veiled widows, our eyes fixing on each other for a breath or two before he turned his attention back to the Mass and to the priest.

But that Sunday, Ramiro wasn't at San Ignacio's.

When my father and I went to greet Padre Andrade by the church doors after the final blessing, I asked where Ramiro had gone.

"We won't be seeing him for a while," Padre Andrade said. And then, as if I should not be surprised, "Our Ramiro has finally answered his calling."

"What do you mean?"

I was worried he'd disappeared back to El Bronx or something worse had happened to him.

"He's gone to the seminary. Ramiro is studying to become a priest."

My father let out an exaggerated gasp. "You really did God's work on that kid, Padre."

"And you, Chana?" Padre Andrade placed a hand on my shoulder, nudging me out of my stunned silence. "What will you become?"

"I don't know."

I had no idea, as my father wished Padre Andrade a good day and watched as the priest gently traced his finger over my forehead in the lines of a cross, that he'd already arranged to have me taken away. They would come for me hours later as I lay on my bed trying to remember Ramiro's face, thinking that like him, I too might be able to break away and change everything about my life, that I could start right now instead of waiting for that distant day when my mother might finally send for me. That Sunday morning, on the church steps, for reasons that seem foolish to me now, even though I had no answer to Padre Andrade's question of what was ahead for me, with Ramiro on my mind, I was full of hope.

THE BONES OF
CRISTÓBAL COLÓN

The caretaker calls from the cemetery to tell me Joaquin's skull and most of his larger and longer bones are missing, but the thieves left some smaller pieces in his grave and I should come by later this morning to collect them.

He says he was the one who made the discovery at dawn.

"The police have already come and gone. They say there is nothing they can do. None of the guards saw anything and nobody knows where to begin a search for stolen bones."

I drop the mop I've been pushing around the cracked floor tiles of the apartment, our peeling blue walls slashed and embered with sunlight.

"I thought my brother would be safe there," I say. "The only way into the Colón is through the gates or over the twelve-foot wall."

"No one is safe from this world's horrors, mi señora."

"But Joaquin's grave is only a few meters from the chapel and the main guard post. How could this happen? There is supposed to be dignity in death."

"You are right, but we should not be so surprised, mi señora. There is always a risk on this island when it comes to bones. Your brother was, after all, a holy man."

I finish washing the floor before leaving for the cemetery. I can't bring my brother home to a place of filth. I feel La Virgen Desatanudos watch me from the altar our mother made for her on a corner table long ago, the porcelain statue set behind a glass bowl habitually filled with sugar water and coins, never flowers, because my mother believed flowers inside the house invite death.

I dust off the Virgin and rearrange the photos at her feet of our family's deceased. *Pray to the Virgin and she will undo all of life's knots,* my mother would say, but it always seemed to me that miniature woman cloaked in red and blue only brought us new ones.

•

Tourists who've come to see the great tombs of Havana's city of the dead watch me pull what is left of Joaquin from the hard soil, pushing away worms. I choke on air pregnant with dirt particles. I cover my mouth with my hand as I sift through my brother's sarcophagus.

The caretaker, a small man of about eighty whom they call Chino, says the thieves must have come hours before first light, when cemetery guards take naps instead of patrolling. He found the stone slab shattered into three pieces and pushed off my brother's tomb. Left behind are small bones that could be mistaken for rocks, smooth and jagged. I place them in the basket I normally use for the market along with a shred of white cloth I find in the soil from the shirt we dressed Joaquin in for his burial.

I wanted to have my brother cremated but our mother said it went against the code of living and dying. A man as good as Joaquin should never have to face flames, she said, especially when we have a good family plot, six generations old, still carrying our last name when the revolution has erased it from everything else that once belonged to our clan. Our mother's grave, a gray concrete sheet set between her son and her husband, is still new, yet to be stained by the coming summer rain.

A young cemetery guard comes by to offer condolences.

"I am very sorry. You must feel as if your brother has died twice."

I recognize him by the thick beaded bracelet he wears for Changó. On one of my weekly visits to lay flowers at my brother's and parents' headstones, I passed a family mausoleum, its iron door propped open by a shovel. Inside, this same young guard lay stretched on a tomb as if it were a bed, taking a nap.

I remember it was on one of the slim arteries off the road to the cemetery chapel. I'd gone there looking for the statue of Amelia La Milagrosa, to touch her hand and the baby in her arms, circle her tomb backward, and ask for blessings in love.

Farther down the road I saw other open mausoleums made into storage sheds, where another two young guards sat on buckets around a raised flat grave, using it as a table on which to have their lunch.

The year my brother was ordained, the priest at a parish in Regla was murdered for his poor box by the married couple that worked as the church's custodians.

His replacement priest died of a heart attack shortly after his arrival.

A few months later, a Spanish priest who ministered to prisoners and the insane was burned alive in his car and left on the side of a road near Bauta.

They don't send you to a labor camp for being a religious anymore, but people still say it's bad luck to be a priest in Cuba.

Joaquin had a career as a government lawyer until he joined the first seminary that opened since before the revolution. He was ordained at forty-five, a man of the cloth for one year until his death.

Our mother said he was poisoned. Joaquin, a child who was never sick, who resisted every virus and plague that hit the tropics, even as I lay ill for months with dysentery or infections in the bedroom we shared. He died of what the doctor called an amoeba, probably from eating dirty beans or rotten pork. His face whitened, his skin thickened, sweating so much that the sheets slid off his bed.

His voice faded, his eyes blackened, and in his last days, he could not see or speak. We whispered to him. We sang to him.

Our mother told him our father was waiting for him in heaven. He died young too, from a brain tumor that stole his memory and movement before finally taking him, though our mother said it was a gift because he wasn't aware that he was dying.

•

Once home, I hold my brother's bones in my lap and call his former parish, where he served until his death, to see if they will offer him a place of rest, but they don't want him. The new priest says if the Paleros who took his remains find out they're in the business of burying holy men on their grounds, the church will become a target of bone theft too.

I call a dozen more churches, some far beyond city limits. Most claim their land is already overcrowded with the dead, their plots already stacked with two or three coffins.

"I just need a corner for my brother's bones. There's not much of him left."

"You have our sympathy, compañera, but there is a waitlist for every centimeter of our soil."

"He was a good man. He did not deserve this fate. Please help us."

Only two or three churches say they will consider my request and let me know.

The revolution created shortages of every kind: food, medicine, housing for the living and the dead, and, especially, a shortage of faith. But our mother said faith is a wave that recedes and returns, as sure as the tide forever threatening to swallow our island.

I place Joaquin's basket of fragments on the altar beside La Virgen Desatanudos so she'll look after his bones and undo the knot of finding a place to bury my brother's remains. It's what my mother would want. She would say there is no place for bones but in the earth.

I open a bottle of rum and pour a glass for my brother and one for the Virgin. I pour another for myself, sit on a chair across from the altar, and drink my rum all at once. It warms me, creates a buzz in my ear that echoes through the apartment, mingles with the talk and traffic rising off Calle Neptuno and the clattering labyrinth of Centro Habana.

I pour another glass. Then another.

•

When the phone rings a few hours later, I expect it to be a nun or a priest with news. I have not moved from the chair. If my mother were here she would be making promises, striking deals with the saints to get what she wants, perhaps offering three hours a day for the rest of her life on her knees before the altar, or volunteering me, her only daughter, to be a nun, to replace her lost son as a servant of God, the way she encouraged me to do since I gave up working because all jobs pay the same around here—essentially nothing. But I make no such promises.

"Ana."

A male voice, as familiar to me as my brother's.

"Yes, it's me."

"I know it's you."

He laughs soft, nervous. This is how I am certain it is Marco.

"I'm in Havana. I hoped you would see me."

My voice has fallen far into me, blocked by the eleven years since we last spoke.

I listen for sounds behind his voice, but there is only silence. From my end, he can surely hear the noises from the street below my windows, the upstairs neighbors banging away on the barbacoa they're constructing to make more room for their family.

"Ana. Are you there?"

"Yes."

"It's not my intention to disrupt your life or to cause you any problems. So many years have passed. But I want to see you. Just to talk to you. I won't take much of your time. Will you meet me this afternoon after you finish work?"

I don't tell him I haven't had a job in years.

"Yes. I'll see you."

"Come to the Triton at five o'clock. I'll wait for you on one of the stone benches by the water. Promise me you'll come, Ana."

"I promise," I say, and pour myself another glass of rum.

•

The first time my brother had to preside over a funeral was at the cemetery in La Lisa. A family was burying their father in a community grave along the wall separating the cemetery from a tin and clapboard slum because there was no money for something better. Joaquin told me there were no flowers in this cemetery, no caretakers to pull the weeds and clear the garbage, and no guards protecting the graves where feuds and rivalries between families were regularly settled by vandalizing each other's plots, revenge found in the splitting of headstones. Some grave slabs were broken, others painted with symbols, and others covered in blood or chicken bones.

The rumor was that most of La Lisa's graves were already empty.

It was nothing like the Colón cemetery, Joaquin said. So beautiful, with its immense statues, soaring winged angels, mausoleums the size of houses; a concrete Garden of Eden where we'd be fortunate to be buried even though we believed our deaths a long way off.

Then he told me how Cristóbal Colón himself has never been laid fully to rest. His bones went from Spain to Santo Domingo, then here to Havana, and back to Spain, an unending international battle to claim his remains.

Nobody knows for sure where his bones are now.

In death, the great colonizer was left without country.

Joaquin and I laughed about this.

It wasn't uncommon to hear of a grave being robbed. Sometimes entire burial plots were stolen; resold after it was determined they'd had no visitors for a decade or two. And when the descendants of the deceased returned to the patria from wherever they'd taken their exile, they'd find their names scratched from the headstones, new names and new corpses in their ancestors' place.

We also heard stories, because there were so many, of graves being ransacked by Paleros, not for whatever treasures coffins may hold but for bones; human feet to make their spells chase and catch their victims, a skull with which to give the spells wisdom and intelligence, hands so that a spell may reach and take hold with the force of a fist. The most coveted bones belonged to esteemed, wealthy, or high-ranking citizens. But the most precious bones of all to procure were those of a man of God, especially that of a bishop or a cardinal, but since those were so few, the bones of any priest would do.

I teased Joaquin that now that he was a priest his bones would be worth more than that of the average cadaver. Paleros and grave thieves would fight over his skeleton just like countries fought over the bones of Cristóbal Colón.

But he insisted he would be safe in the cemetery.

"No grave thief with any sense would bother with bones of a late-ordained priest whose own sister falls asleep during his sermons," Joaquin told me. "I may have been called to serve the Lord, Anita, but I am no holy man."

•

There are three hours between Marco and me. I am still filthy from my brother's excavation. I shower, carve the dirt out from under my nails, and examine myself in the mirror to see how I have changed. Marco will compare me to the Ana he knew at thirty-three, the Ana he left. The Ana who did more with her days than sit around playing cards with herself, shuffling between the neighbors' apartments where we talk only about those who have left the island, wondering what their lives are like now. I wear the same dresses I did then, my hair in the same cropped side-part style. I wear the same jewelry; pieces inherited from my mother, left to her by her mother, among the few things our family held on to rather than sell, even during our hungriest years. But my eyes have surely dropped; my skin has certainly thinned. My body has softened, and my curves have flattened. I want to be beautiful today but even after two showers, I feel I still smell of death.

I see us there on the beach by the Tropicoco hotel, Marco's last day in Cuba though he had not yet told me so. He'd left me for another woman two years earlier but still saw me, still told me in his heart I was the only one, and when I asked why he'd chosen another he said these were things I'd never understand because I am a woman.

And I said, "Because I am a woman, there are things I understand that you never will until it is too late. You will regret having left me. You will wonder all your life if you chose wrong. You will be haunted and unable to feel peace in your heart. The moments in which you hate your life with her will grow and multiply, and you will doubt any child she gives you because it was not born from me, from you, from us."

We were hot on a blanket he'd brought for us, cradled by the soft sand. He watched me speak. He nodded. He said he believed me. But it didn't change anything. He'd already decided.

The next day I wondered why he hadn't called as he normally did. My mother said he'd finally had the integrity to stand by one woman and leave me alone. My brother comforted me as I cried. He later came to me with the news a neighbor passed on: Marco had left the island with her. They'd gone to Ecuador, where she had family, where they planned to start a new life even if it meant never coming back.

•

The botero ruta is congested. I have to wait for a spot in a taxi, and it takes three car changes to get me to the Triton. I see Marco, his body turned to the ocean, waves smashing over rocks and rolling onto the concrete walkway lined with benches. He turns as if I've called his name, though I haven't. He walks toward me, still tall but wider and thicker than when he left. I feel I've shrunken when we are before each other. He leans to kiss my cheek as if we are distant cousins. I avoid his eyes. I don't want him to see I am crumbling.

We sit on a bench. He's brought a small bottle of rum with him and offers me some, which I take, though I am already swaying.

Marco notices. "Ana, are you drunk?"

I shake my head, then nod. "A little bit."

I tell him the Paleros stole my brother's bones from the cemetery last night and I had to collect the bits they left behind this morning.

"Dios santo," he whispers. "I didn't know your brother died. How is your mother handling it?"

"She died too. Two months after him. Pneumonia."

"Oh, Ana. I don't have words."

He can say he is sorry to hear it. Or he can say what we know to be true: long before he abandoned me for her and for Ecuador, Marco told me he wanted to leave this island and asked if we could find a way to do it together.

I said I could never leave my brother and my mother. I didn't believe in the fracturing of families in the name of immigration; I didn't believe the myth that a better life awaited elsewhere. I believed we were born to our island no matter its fate, and our duty was to make the best of it, offering it our lives, even if it means we are the ones who are sacrificed.

In the years since, I would look back on that conversation and blame it for our undoing, blame myself for my rigidity, then blame my brother and mother, for leaving me here alone.

Instead Marco tells me this is his first trip back since he left eleven years ago. He is a citizen of Ecuador now. He lives in Guayaquil where he manages a Cuban restaurant. He has traveled to Panama, Colombia, Argentina, Peru, and Chile.

"I hope you get to travel somewhere someday, Ana. You'll see any place is better than here."

But then, as swiftly as a cloud covers the sun, his face changes from bravado to melancholy.

"I do miss this coast though. Where I live I see the Pacific, but it's not the same. I miss our currents. I miss our beaches. I miss our place by the Tropicoco."

He slips his hand under mine so that our palms press together.

"Will you go with me somewhere?"

"Where?"

"Someplace beautiful. Someplace you've never been."

He has a car he's rented. A modern French model with air-conditioning and an electronic radio. I push the buttons while he drives down the Malecón, but all the stations play the same boring music.

"You can't imagine how it is outside of this island," he says. "More radio stations and television stations than a person could watch or listen to in a lifetime. You can never get bored of anything."

He parks the car by the Parque Central and leads me to one of the hotels on its periphery, behind huge Yutong tour buses, through a lobby crowded with foreigners.

We go into an elevator and when we come out we are on the roof of the building, Havana spread out below us, broken buildings and plastered-on azoteas, mosaics of flesh tones and muted blues, an Atlantic breeze curling around us, dividing us from the noise below.

There is a swimming pool and a restaurant up here, and many foreign men having drinks with what look to me to be young Cuban women.

Marco leans against the wall, and I stand beside him.

"You look lovely in this light. Just as I remember you."

He touches my face, the same way he did the night we met. It was at a party, when I used to go to parties. He found me in a corner and asked me why I looked so serious. "I bet I can make you smile,"

he said, touching my face, then lightly kissing my cheek, and before I
could think to ask why he'd done that, he'd gone for my lips.

He touches my face and kisses my cheek, then my lips.

I think this cannot be. I am not here. I am still in my home, before
the Virgin's altar, staring at my brother's bones, small and white as
seashells.

"Ana, how is it that I feel no time has passed between us? I feel the
same today as I did the night I met you and every day until the last
time we saw each other."

I cannot speak, I only hope this is the moment I have begged for:
Marco's return to me.

"Tell me," he says. "Do you feel the same way?"

I say yes, because a morning spent digging in my brother's grave,
beside my parents' tombs, must mean this could be my last evening
on earth.

•

When Joaquin lay dying, a young woman often came to see him. She
sat at his side and looked at him tenderly while he could still see, and
when he lost his sight, she would cry silently into his bedsheets.

"Who is she?" I asked my mother and then the ladies of the parish
office, but nobody would give an answer. It was the church janitor
who told me the woman, twice divorced and childless, came to my
brother for almost daily counsel.

My brother's last sermon before falling sick was about how God
rewards the just. We must not give into temptation. We are sinners
and by sinning we will fall.

The woman came to the burial, and before she left, I stopped her
and asked her to remind me, because my memory was hazy, how it
was she came to know Joaquin.

"I was in love with your brother."

I suspected this much but was still surprised she didn't lie to me.

"Was he in love with you?"

"I don't know."

I never told my mother. She wanted to believe Joaquin pious, not a new priest struggling with the worldly delights he vowed to leave behind. *Joaquin is a man of divine grace, Ana*, she would say. *He is not weak, like you.*

•

Marco has a room in this hotel. This is why he brought me here. He admits he has been in Havana a week and stayed with his parents. He told them he was leaving last night and even had them take him to the airport for a teary farewell. Instead he went to the ticket counter and changed his departure for two days later. When he was sure his family was gone, he left the terminal, took a taxi back to the city, checked into the hotel and waited until morning to call me.

"Why did you wait until morning?" I ask.

"I wanted to be sure."

"And are you?"

"Yes."

We are in his hotel room, with a small balcony overlooking the park.

I sit on the small sofa near the window, and Marco, on the edge of the bed facing me.

"Come sit by me, Ana."

I shake my head.

"You're anxious."

"A bit."

He sips more rum and passes me the bottle.

"Have you ever been in a hotel room this nice?"

"Yes," I say, which is true. With a man I met not long after Marco left, a Spaniard I forced myself to sleep with on the first night as an antidote to the loss.

In those days it was easier to meet men. I was a teller at the Casa de Cambio on Obispo and just on the walk from home to work and back, I'd meet a man or two on the street. But around age forty, it was as if the lipstick I put on each morning made me invisible.

I thought I would find a man to marry after Marco. Most of the women I know marry two or three times, at least once for love, and maybe again, for convenience, companionship, or opportunity. I didn't expect my future would open wide into nothing.

Since I won't go to him, Marco comes to me, sits on the small sofa, which is not very comfortable, sliding his hands around me. He kisses me, and I let him. We are both drunk, but it doesn't matter.

Eleven years that felt like sleep, I think, closing my eyes, just as he tells me he has waited for this night for so long and lived it already many times in his dreams.

In bed, he is more commanding than I remember, perhaps because he is heavier now, dense and crushing as he pushes into me, yet we are familiar to each other as if we never parted, as if he were mine all along.

We lie together afterward, the bed warm as if we are still on the sand by the Tropicoco, under the summer sun, as young as when we met, still limber, still intoxicated by the uncharted future.

He speaks into my shoulder.

"Everything is as you said it would be."

"What do you mean?"

"You said I would never be able to stop thinking of you. You said I would always wonder if I made the right choice in leaving you. You said I would love no one as I loved you. You were right about everything."

•

Marco's wife has always known about me. He was careless. He left letters I'd written him around the room they shared in her parents' house. These were letters in which I'd pleaded for him to be with only me, saying I didn't understand why he'd decided we were an impossibility, when we agreed our connection was both primal and otherworldly. Among the papers were letters he'd drafted to me, describing nights we'd stolen away up to an azotea, or to an empty beach on the city outskirts, anywhere we could go to be alone; letters in which he told me he could not leave me no matter how hard he willed it, that even if the world saw him with her, he would always be with me.

She would not abandon him but she forbade him from seeing me. For a few months, he obeyed, and left me to wander through Centro Habana, my face the color of the deteriorating concrete walls, eyes sullen, and heart pitted by his desertion.

Until he came back to me.

Giving me up was the hardest thing he'd had to do in all his life, he'd said. So hard that he would never be able to do it again.

Until he left our island.

We are deep into the night, resisting sleep in order to keep every moment of our shared darkness alive.

"Marco. How is it that she let you come back to Cuba alone?"

It's been eleven years, but she must have known the risk.

"She didn't let me. She came with me."

When they were already at the airport, about to pass the security point to wait for their flight, he begged his wife for one more night in Havana. He needed more time with his family. She had to get back to her job, so he knew she couldn't stay too.

"I even cried," he says in this new version. "They were real tears. I told her to give me one more day and I would be on a plane to Ecuador tomorrow. I said, 'I followed you to another country. Let me have one more day in mine.' She finally agreed to leave alone."

My brother used to say Marco was the worst kind of liar, because he manages to be dishonest even when he's telling the truth.

·

In the morning, Marco and I eat breakfast together in the hotel restaurant. There is food spread on a long counter, more than I have ever seen in one place. Hot food, cold food; piles of bread, bowls of fruits, platters of cooked eggs, and every kind of cold meat.

Marco laughs at me as I take it in.

"It's a buffet. You can fill your plate and come back for more as many times as you want."

We sit at a table for two by the window. At other small tables I see more foreign men with girls, faces wiped clean of last night's makeup.

"Look at us," Marco says. "When I left the island, it was still against the law for Cubans to stay in hotels."

I chew buttery bread that melts on my tongue, more delicious than anything I have ever tasted.

"Things are changing," Marco says, though to me nothing has changed.

When I leave this hotel I will be hungry again, but there will be no boundless buffet waiting for me. There will be only the food of the ration card, what is left in the markets, what I'm able to purchase with whatever little money I have.

"You can even buy and sell property now," he says, as if I am the only Cuban at this table. "Of course few have the money for that but it's still a big change that you now have the right."

I bite into a piece of cooked dough with a burst of chocolate inside that slides onto my tongue, so creamy and rich I almost tremble.

"We're thinking of buying an apartment here to use for vacations. We can rent it to tourists when we're not using it. It will be an investment."

I don't remember ever eating with such pleasure, such novelty.

He watches me. When I finish my bacon, my plate clear, and put down my fork, Marco asks if I've been listening.

"Of course."

"So what do you think?"

"You watch Cuba like a movie on one of your TV channels. From far away, you see *changes*. If you'd stayed here, you would see life is the same as it has always been."

"I'm trying to tell you I'll be coming back here more often."

"For vacations. I heard you."

He shakes his head. "You don't understand, Ana. It's all for you. I have been waiting for this day. Eleven years won't pass again. We're not young anymore. We don't have as much time ahead of us as we'd like to think."

"You don't have to tell me that."

•

He insists on driving me home on his way to the airport even after I tell him I can walk. Every time we pause at a red light, he leans over to kiss me. When we arrive on Neptuno, I ask him to come upstairs for a minute. It's been so long since he's walked within my walls. We used to avoid my home because my mother and brother were there. He leaves the car by the curb and asks the children sitting in the doorway of a building across the road to look after it. He is no longer accustomed to the routine of climbing so many flights of stairs. His face is red by the time we reach my door.

The apartment is cast in greenish morning light, the rings of Joaquin's and the Virgin's rum glasses reflecting halos on the walls.

I lead Marco to the table holding the Virgin, and show him the basket containing my brother's bones.

"May he rest in peace," Marco says, making the sign of the cross.

"That's a stupid thing to say when obviously he didn't."

"I'm sorry. I don't know what else to say in a case like this."

"You know, my brother never liked you. He said you have no character. He said you are incapable of being happy because you are so greedy. You want it all, but what you have right in front of you is never good enough."

Marco is surprised but nods.

"Your brother was a smart man."

"You had to leave your country in order to leave me."

"I know."

"The only reason you've managed to stay married is because there is a sea between us."

"I know."

"Aren't you even going to argue with me? Tell me I'm wrong."

He shakes his head. "No, Ana. Everything you say is true."

•

I sit on the chair and face Joaquin and the Virgin.

I can feel my brother's simultaneous disapproval and mercy.

The telephone rings, and I hear a woman's voice.

"This is Graciela," she says. "You may not remember me. I came to see your brother when he was ill. I heard what happened to him at the cemetery."

She confesses she's stopped going to Mass since my brother died. She's had a crisis of faith. She doesn't know what she believes anymore. But a woman from her apartment building works in the rectory of a church in El Romerillo, a half-abandoned and very poor parish.

"The priest says Joaquin's bones are welcome to rest there, and they promise to look after them."

One knot undone.

"Joaquin," I whisper to his bones when I hang up the phone, "I'm going to drink your rum for you and then I'm going to deliver you to your new home."

I take his rum into my mouth, but I don't touch the Virgin's.

•

"Tell me one last bit of truth," Marco said to me before he left me in my doorway.

"What truth?"

"Tell me you haven't loved anyone since you loved me."

"If I told you that, it wouldn't be true."

"Then tell me you loved me best. Despite what we are. Despite what I've done to you."

"I have loved you best. Despite what we are. Despite what you've done to me." I separated myself from him, stepping backward into the apartment. "But Ecuador is your country now."

He moved forward, pulling me into another embrace.

"This will always be my country. My island will always be you."

We kiss and kiss, and I feel as if we are being buried alive together.

•

An old priest welcomes me into the church in El Romerillo. He is small and pale and bald, with pink spots of cancer and burned moles on his forehead and neck and hands.

Graciela is here too, slimmer than I remember her, in a long lavender dress, as if she's here to attend a wedding.

The priest takes us to a small garden behind the church. We walk along the brick ledge where he has already made a hole and set within it a wooden box, its lid removed.

I take the bones from the basket and the scraps of cloth that remain in my hands, remembering the dirt I struggled to wash off my fingers, and regret that I didn't let the stains wear on me a little longer.

I cover the box with the lid, and the priest recites some prayers for my brother.

Graciela weeps. I can't help but reach for her hand.

After we cover the box with soil and the priest sprinkles it with holy water, giving the final blessing, he motions to the naked earth around us and tells us this garden looks empty but is full of shards of bone from tombs robbed all over Havana, rescued and given refuge here.

He tells us he was ordained as a young man, before the revolution, and has seen this island through its many incarnations. He has had opportunities to leave. He has family abroad who invited him to live with them. He has traveled to Europe and all over the Americas. He has had many chances to defect but he always returned to his country.

"Padre, why did you choose to stay?" I ask.

The priest looks to Graciela and to me, then to the ground where we've just buried Joaquin.

"Because I could not bear the thought of dying somewhere else."

When I return home, I find my apartment eclipsed by nightfall. I think of Marco, in a place so far away I cannot even imagine it, yet somehow, still here with me, so close I can taste him, as if our night never ended and I've not been sentenced once again to waiting.

I think of my brother's bones, tiny pieces in the priest's bare garden, the rest of him likely already set in a pot, buried in a forest waiting to be put to work by his new masters.

I think of the bits of him left in this home; clothes, books, photographs, letters to our mother and me. I think of my mother, grateful that she did not live to handle her son's bones the way I have, to feel the final remnants of his existence as minerals on her fingertips.

LIBÉLULA

1

THE FIRST TIME WE MET YOU ASKED ME TO TEA. IT WAS AT AN ITALIAN bakery not far from where you lived. You ordered for me. A cappuccino and a chocolate pastry. You didn't want me to see your home yet. You confessed that later, months after you'd offered me the job to clean and supplement care for the baby you planned to have, though you said you would also hire a nanny. You complimented my sweater and my nails. You asked if I painted them myself, and when I told you I did, you said you'd pay me extra to do yours too.

We were the same age but you spoke as if much older, as if I were a child and you were my educator. You explained the neighborhood. When you showed me around your apartment a few days later, you presented your park view as if it were a blue blood family crest. Your husband was traveling. I would not meet him for several more weeks, but he participated in our discussions when you told me he liked his boxers ironed, his collars pinned, his shoes sorted according to hue.

You'd met in infancy, you said. Your families knew each other for generations. You came to this country together for university and were permitted to live together with the understanding that you'd marry after graduation and you both complied.

In another life, I might have also been your maid back in Colombia. You might have inherited me from your mother, who employed my mother, or I might have arrived at your door referred by one of my friends who was employed by one of yours. I also came to this country with a man who pledged to marry me. In the end I was the one who escaped vows and he returned to Medellín because this country did not deliver on its promises. I didn't say any of this when you hired me. You only knew I'd been employed as a housekeeper for years by a Swiss family on the west side who'd relocated to Dubai. You wanted someone to work full-time, the way it was when you were growing up. Not a once-a-week cleaner as was common around here. You wanted a woman to be there when you woke up, to serve your breakfast on the dining room table and disappear in the evening when your husband returned from work and you would wait for him at the same table in an outfit you modeled for me earlier, asking if it was obvious you'd gained a few pounds. You wanted a ghost, a shadow to move about your home anticipating your every need. A double as loyal as an imaginary friend to accompany you, potentially until your death when I'd be retired and returned to my relatives. This proposal did not offend me because I was raised as you were, but on the other side of such an arrangement, and, as you assured me when you offered me the position, I would be well compensated.

2

You did not work and felt no shame about it. You were too busy to have a job, you said; you barely had enough time to get the sleep you needed with all your errands and appointments. You'd studied finance, but your husband managed your money and his secretary called sometimes to go over charges on the credit card statements. You gave me cash and a pushcart for grocery shopping. You liked for me to go to the market every day as if we lived in Europe, you said, or back home where the produce was fresh and not waxed and lifeless as it is here. I cooked for you, though you complained my recipes were too simple. Beans, you said, were peasant food. You bought me cookbooks. You positioned me in front of the television to watch instructional programs of famous chefs. I was not a very good student and rotated the same few dishes I'd mastered every week. But I did your manicures and pedicures, massaged your shoulders, and brushed your hair as you told me your husband was a reluctant lover, that his mother secretly despised you and you secretly despised her; that if you didn't have a baby soon you feared he would leave you and you'd have nowhere to go but back to Colombia and you would rather die than return to your family without a husband or a child to show for your time abroad. I listened with the devotion of a nun and so you let me stay.

I came to this country at twenty-three. The same year you married. My boyfriend was already here, working as a doorman in Long Island City. We rented an efficiency near St. Michael's Cemetery, and I found a job cleaning tables and counters in a cafeteria. When things turned bad with him, I went to live with a friend on Lamont Avenue. She was the one who told me about La Palmera, the dollar club on Roosevelt. Everyone does it at some point, she said. Harmless, fast cash. All I needed to do was wear party clothes and high heels and sit along the wall with the other women until a man asked me to dance. Two dollars a song. Forty dollars if he could commit to a whole hour. The men were mostly day laborers, rough-handed, often still in their work clothes. They would ask me to dance, and it was like in the old days you hear older people describe when everyone was well-mannered, when a dance and holding hands had nothing to do with sex. This is how it was until one of those men became aggressive or obsessive with one of the ladies, which happened from time to time, confusing payment with romance.

There were security guards who looked out for us. The truth is I had no bad experiences there. It was a safe place for me, dark and full of lonely strangers who felt moved by human touch and conversation over cheap beer and watered-down cocktails. These men spoke of wives and children they left in their countries, wondering if there would ever be enough money to bring them over or to justify the end of their American experiment and go back home themselves. Sometimes the men didn't pay, so I started collecting my cash before going to the dance floor the way a prostitute would do, though I did not see dancing for dollars as prostitution. Still, it was nothing I would ever tell anyone, even my mother, and especially you. But I came to see time as the measure of a song on a scale of money, and in my future jobs, I'd see my tasks as a series of tunes, the washing of dishes, the folding of laundry, the making of beds equivalent to a set of salsa or bachata.

3

I ran into a friend at El Mundo supermarket who told me about a studio share available in Manhattan. The apartment belonged to a woman who worked as a live-in nanny and used it only on weekends when the family didn't want her around. I could sleep in the bed all week, and take the sofa on Saturdays and Sundays. She was the one who set me up with the family that led me to you. When I told you I lived up on 177th Street, you made it sound like Canada. You could not believe I took two trains and a bus to reach you all before you woke up each morning. You hated the subway. The bus was even worse. You could tolerate taxis if your life depended on it, but your preferred mode of transportation was a chauffeured car from the service your husband's company supplied without end. When you had the first miscarriage, you preferred to wait for the driver instead of taking one of the dozen yellow cabs that passed in front of the building. You folded into yourself. I held you by the elbow so you wouldn't spill to the ground. I'd helped you pad your underwear for the bleeding. You whimpered in pain. Your husband said he would meet you at the doctor but it was two hours of you splayed on the table releasing tissue before he arrived. You asked me to stay with you. You held my hand and your eyes found mine when they weren't pressed shut. The doctor came in between other patients. Better to be here than in the hospital, he said. If you were lucky, your body would complete the process naturally and you wouldn't need surgery. When he stepped out you repeated his words. *If you're lucky.* I hated him for you, and your husband even more when he did show up, for the way he kept turning from you, checking his phone, groaning as if his body were expelling a life and not yours.

When we took you home, you asked that I remain in your room with you and not your husband, who did not protest. You begged me to stay the night. You would pay me extra, you said, and I told you there was no need. I stroked your forehead as you fell into the kind of sleep I know was not restful. You were in another dimension, one I recognized from the time I lost a pregnancy, though for me it was a relief more than a sorrow because the man I was with at the time did not want to be a father, but the ache was just as morbid, the void, undeniable. In the morning your husband found me sleeping on his half of the bed. I stood up, embarrassed, but he did not look my way; to him I was as invisible as ever, his wife's little doll, I presume. He kissed your brow and apologized for having to go to work. You did not respond. Your eyes said you loathed him. We both did. That morning, the room diffused in gray light, we were the same.

4

Your new home was a narrow brownstone with a designated servant's quarters behind the kitchen. You told me I would have my own bathroom and private entrance. You didn't expect I'd hesitate to leave my current living situation uptown for your address on the southeast end of Central Park. You did not know I was in love at the time with a man who lived a few doors down from the apartment I shared with the other woman. He lived with his wife and her mother and his mother in the sort of communal misery that can only flourish when you have a family you so love. I was careless and forlorn in the way that the men who paid for dances with me were, so eager for a soft touch, for eyes that did not judge. To him, I was just another solitary woman in the neighborhood. We slept together many times at my place. He was quick and generally took me from behind, then went home to his family. I did not know how to stop desiring him, so when you proposed that I come live with you and that you would increase my pay accordingly, I agreed.

You were hopeful you would get pregnant again, even as months passed without a sign. You changed doctors many times. You gave blood and took pills and started diets to help your fertility. Women came to the house to massage and push pins into you, to teach you poses and hypnotize you into motherhood. You kept a thermometer and a calendar by the bed where you marked certain days with a purple pen. And then you were pregnant. You showed me the pale line on a plastic stick, and for the rest of the day urinated on several more and displayed them on the counter to show your husband when he came home. Over dinner you asked him why he didn't seem happy. He wanted to be cautious, he said. He was afraid you'd both end up disappointed like last time. I was in the kitchen cleaning when you met me by the counter with a wet-eyed stare. My bedroom was two flights below yours, but the house was old and I heard your fights through the vents, how you pleaded for some emotion and how he called you irrational, demanding, and depressing to look at. The next day, the pink streak on the sticks was gone. The phantasm of a pregnancy departed, and you moved about the house stiffly. You stood at the doorway to the room you'd outfitted with a crib because one of the experts you hired told you it was the way to manifest your desired outcome. I put my hand on your shoulder, and you turned into me so that we were embracing in a way I did not expect and never would have initiated because I know such intimacy cannot be tolerated in a workplace, even among those employers who claim their domestics are like family. But you held me, and I felt the absence of your mother and your sisters and my mother and my sisters, and when you finally pulled away you apologized as if you'd done something terrible and went to your room.

That night I was in bed watching the television you gave me as I did most nights. You had all the premium Spanish channels, so I could keep up with telenovelas and programs my mother was watching back home and we could text each other about it during the day. I remember we were watching a true-crime series about a group of rich teenagers who murder a lower-class schoolmate. It was representative of all our country's injustices and inequalities, my mother said. I preferred these shows to ones with romantic plotlines that only made my body feel more ravenous and abandoned. That night's episode was to be of the courtroom trial. I was looking forward to the prosecutor's opening remarks. But then the door opened and your husband showed his face, put his finger to his lips, and stepped through. I pulled the blanket over my breasts, which hung braless in a T-shirt, and since I was in my own room, I didn't bother wearing pants, but your husband could not know this. I asked if something was wrong. I thought he would talk about you, ask if we could plan a special surprise to cheer you up. Maybe he had an idea to take you on vacation or on one of his work trips like you were always begging him to do. He watched me, and I noticed he was growing hard, as if by the air, and I didn't know what to say or do, and I have no way to explain what happened next; I can merely tell you the facts, which are that he came to my bed without speaking, pulled the blanket off me and saw only my underwear separating my skin from the sheets and quickly shoved his hand under the fabric and into me. When I said your name, he answered that you were asleep, so sure that I would not resist beyond worrying you might discover us. The next morning, I served you breakfast at the dining room table with a fresh rose in a bud vase beside your water glass, the way you required, and you could intuit no difference in me and I remembered the ways you did not see me at all, left your clothes strewn about your bedroom, wet towels tossed to the tile, your long hair filling every drain, with no consciousness for the energy it took to bend for you over and over, to expunge your filth. In your mind you were perfect, and I helped offer that notion to everyone who entered your home, to those who heard you talk about all the care you put into your household upkeep. When a magazine came to photograph your home, you did not show them my room and told me to leave the house for the afternoon. Americans don't understand how we are about employing houseworkers, you said. They think everything is exploitation. Then you wanted my opinion. You like working here, don't you? We treat you well, don't we? I nodded. Of course, I said. You didn't insist that I call you señora or doña. You said I could call you by only your first name and when you took me around the city on your shopping excursions, you referred to me as your friend to salespeople and waiters when we stopped for lunch, even as you criticized my table manners or corrected the way I spoke, mocking my idioms. You gave me clothes you no longer wanted even if they still fit you and were like new. In fact, on many nights when your husband came to my room after you were sleeping, I was wearing a nightgown that had once been yours.

5

You never thought me beautiful, and why should you? I am not. When my boyfriend was unfaithful I learned the other woman doesn't need to be prettier, she only needs to be different. You noticed your husband leaving your room some nights and mentioned it to me. You thought he was going to the den to watch television or to play computer games since he knew the screen light bothered you. You were deep into your fertility treatments and cried most afternoons and iced your face to depuff before dinner. You went through many cycles that produced no good embryos. You were one of five children. Your parents, each one of eight. You didn't know what you did to be cursed with unwilling ovaries and a bully uterus. You asked me to go with you to see a brujo uptown who wore a robe and sat on a golden throne. He said you would have four pregnancies. When you replied that you'd already miscarried four times, he added nothing more.

On the way home we stopped in a church and you asked a priest sweeping the altar for a blessing, and he gave me one too. We dipped into the park before crossing the avenue to the house. The weather was calm and bright, and the city was curiously quiet. We lay on the grass like schoolgirls, and I thought of the years before I understood I would have to work every day in a home and that this meant I'd never really have a home of my own. How strange the grass felt in this city, so different from the grass and earth I felt under me in my youth. I asked if when you came to this country for university you knew that you'd stay here forever. You said you never thought so far ahead but you are a citizen now, so that must mean you are an official immigrant. Not me, I said. That word never seemed to fit even though I'd already married for papers and divorced and was as much a citizen as you were. I thought of myself as a satellite sent into orbit and when I'd return to my base on Earth was yet to be determined, though inevitable. Till then I'd remain in transit, circling my planet until I went home or went dead in outer space.

Sundays I typically went to see old friends in Jackson Heights. You encouraged me to socialize with the other housekeepers and nannies of our neighborhood so I wouldn't have to go so far for camaraderie, but then I overheard your mother warn you on a video call that it's not good for maids to talk to other maids because they start comparing notes and next thing you know, you have to give your maid a raise three times a year. I knew I was already overpaid compared to other women who worked in the area. You did not deduct for my room or for providing food. I finally paid off my marriage debt and sent most of my salary to my mother, who was able to move into a new apartment. She wanted me to come home for a month at Christmas now that I could afford a ticket, but you said you would die without me, and besides, you needed someone to watch the house while you went skiing, so I postponed. You were filling out paperwork for adoption. You had an idea that you could adopt from Colombia and maybe it was your fate. Your husband did not want to parent someone else's child. It would be *your* child, you said. I heard it through the vent. I heard it again over breakfast and at dinner. Still, you worked for months on those forms. When your husband came to my room he wanted only to please me. I pretended he was not your husband and this was not your house and I was not your maid or empleada or muchacha or mujer de servicio as you would call me if we were in our own country. Perhaps your husband thrust his virginity upon one such woman in his childhood home. At night I thought of none of those things. It was the only way to forget the songs in my head, the infinite loop waiting for something to change in my life of waged companionship and knowing it would not.

6

I left you because I could not stand to see your dejected face or the way I would make it worse. If I think back, the moments when I saw you content are few. The day when we lay together in the grass and you marveled at a dragonfly that landed on your finger, said it reminded you of the ones floating around the grounds of your family's country house as a girl, that afternoon choosing you over all the human bodies in the park, proclaiming it a spirit marker, an omen of good things to come, and I did not dare tell you that in the barrio of my youth, a libélula touching your skin meant exactly the opposite. Or when I saw you dress for dinner each night with hope that somehow your outfit would draw your husband's soul closer to yours. If you saw me like this, it would destroy you, and I am not a destroyer, so I had to leave you. I waited until you were out with a friend for lunch. The friend you often got drunk with in the middle of the day or at night when your husband was in a different time zone. The European diplomat's wife. You envied the lifestyle her husband's career afforded. The wide embassy town house, the staff of six. You smoked marijuana and did cocaine with only her, you said, because it didn't feel as trashy. I loved handing you off to her because it relieved me of caring for you for a few hours. This day, when you said goodbye and gave me instructions for what to make for dinner, I wished you well and hoped I would never see you again.

When you came home, instead of calling for me to guide your drunken steps up the stairs, to prepare you a hangover preventative, or to ask me to lie to your husband about why you were feeling tired and ill, you would find the house empty. There would be no dinner waiting for you and your husband. You both might search the house, taking inventory of your valuables. The only things in my bag were my clothes, none that you gave me but what I brought with me when I moved into your lives, some money I saved, my marriage and divorce papers and my passports.

I rented a room in Corona from a woman I knew from La Palmera who still danced by the song. She told me I could come too, make some cash like I used to, letting men press their cheeks to mine, but I showed her the soft curve beneath my navel. It's okay, she said. You don't have to drink. Just tell the bartenders to fill your cocktails with juice instead of liquor. Ladies do it all the time, and some dance till their third trimester. I still hadn't figured out where I would land. An American baby, my friend cooed. She didn't ask who the father was. I never would have told her. I've seen enough news programs to know disadvantaged mothers can have their children taken away for putting on a diaper crooked. I had a vision of you mothering the life inside me. And still I did not panic, even as I considered a future where you and I might run into each other in the park or on the avenues we once walked together, me carrying your packages, and you would see the child in my arms, notice a resemblance, do some math, and understand the origin of my motherhood. I would have something that could never be yours.

When my mother asked, I told her the truth that my employer's husband got me pregnant and she let out a revolted sigh but acknowledged that sometimes these things are unavoidable, and such bastardry is so customary in our hemisphere that it's secured a role in all the classic telenovelas. I found work in a restaurant and back at El Mundo I was introduced to a friend's cousin who manages a flower supply. He asked me to ice cream, to a movie, to pizza, and taught me the scientific names for a dozen species of Colombian magnolias before I admitted I had a baby due in a few months and he said he would still like to see me. He was raised in Sincelejo. He has memories of his father hitting a man with his car on a country road and not stopping, even as the children saw in the rearview mirror that the man had been killed. The trauma made him righteous and repentant. I will be your child's father, he said.

7

And then you are before me, not in the way I envisioned but close. We are at JFK at the gate waiting for our flight to Medellín to depart. I am with my husband and son. You are with your husband and daughter. I will never know how your child came to be yours, and you will never know how mine came to be mine. Your husband doesn't even know it, shining ignorance in the way he shakes my husband's hand and congratulates us on our handsome family as if we are lifelong friends, as if the past was swept away by your new maid's broom. My husband welcomes his good wishes, believing my son's father some dishonorable vanished lover.

You hug me, and I feel you warm against my neck. I have missed you, you say. You forgive me, you add, and I wonder for what, since I have not said I am sorry. Early in my employment I tried to quit after you yelled at me for using the wrong liquid on your wood floors. I was already standing at the elevator holding a bag with my few things but you followed me saying everyone makes mistakes and convinced me to stay. I later heard you on the phone with your sister, laughing about how I'd made a show in trying to leave as if I weren't replaceable, as if there weren't ten other women who could do my job for cheaper and with less of an ego. She's so humble yet so prideful, you'd said. And still I loved you. And you loved me. In an incomplete way, of course. Love's imposter twin that still feels real because it has become constant, ordinary, routine. Love doesn't need to be exquisite for it to be true. I learned this with my husband, who is faithful and never punishes me with indifference.

You give me your parents' address in Medellín and say to call so we can get together during our vacations. You'd love to have us over for lunch and show me where you grew up. You could even send their driver to collect us. We watch your family board ahead of everyone, and when it's our turn, we edge through the aisle and see you in your first-class seats, so focused on managing your champagne flutes and the child on your lap that you don't notice us pass. They seem like nice people, my husband says when we take our own seats behind the wing. We don't need to call or see them, I say. He doesn't ask why.

At the luggage claim, your baby is crying, and I am surprised you haven't brought a nanny with you the way you always declared you would to travel. Your baby seems too heavy or your arms too weak. Your husband takes her, holds her close, and she is soothed. Your bags are the first to appear on the conveyor, adorned with priority tags. You wave to us as you make your way to customs and disappear.

I will think of you often for reasons I can't explain. When my son is five, already in school, I will take the train to Manhattan and sit on a bench along the park across the avenue from your house, impatient for proof that you still live there. I will wait for hours until you emerge with your daughter on one hand, your purse in the other, wondering if I will catch your gaze, but you only look ahead, and then you are gone and I never look for you again.

Years later, a vision comes to me as real to me as my own breath: you and I sitting on that plane approaching our shared birth city, my awareness of you so close that I smell your perfume. I recall how a similar jet crashed into the mountains surrounding our valley just a few months earlier, killing everyone on board, the tragedy of the year. I imagine the passengers' fear. I read somewhere that panic comes from lack of preparation. That's why on airplanes they give emergency instructions every time as if it's the first, remind everyone where the escape routes are, and why when you enter a new space you should always locate the exits so a fire doesn't catch you by surprise. Forget instincts, the article said. Survival requires practice and a plan. I close my eyes and see us spiral through the clouds with our families, the raging, rippling Andes biting the side of our plane, leaving no survivors. You and I swallowed and returned to the soil and rock that made us, erasing time and the lives we made in the other world, as if we'd never once dared to wander so far away.

AGUACERO

I REMEMBER THE SKY HAD BEEN DARK SINCE MORNING, AS IF PRO-
testing the start of another day. Rain held off till afternoon, then
started heavy: long, gray water shards dropping on the pavement. I'd
just left my therapist's office without an umbrella and stopped for a
pack of cigarettes in one of those Midtown shops, the size of a closet
and smelling of nuts and tobacco, because nothing makes me want to
smoke more than a visit to the shrink.

I remember the only other customer was a boy of about fifteen
paying for rolling papers and a lottery ticket he told the cashier was
for his mom, and after, I stood outside the shop, my back pressed
against the glass window under the cover of the black awning, trying
to decide if I should make a run for the nearest subway all the way
over on Eighth Avenue. I hated city rain. The kind that sticks to your
face, stiffens your hair, makes you stink like a dog drenched in its own
piss. Nothing like the gentle purifying showers you see out in the
country or by the sea.

One of my cousins in Bogotá once taught me a trick: light a cigarette, hold it out with your hand, and an available taxi will appear, guaranteed.

I opened a flame and extended my cigarette arm to the curb.

For my cousin, the trick never failed. For me, nothing.

I retreated to the shelter of the awning, watching the rain slashes, the glossy street current rush toward the sewers.

"You're Colombian."

This came from a guy I hadn't noticed standing next to me. Something about urban living makes it so you don't even feel when your arm is pressed against a stranger's.

"How would you know?"

I didn't speak much in those days unless I had to, so my own voice sounded strange, defensive, even to me.

"You have an Andean face. Also, you just tried to call a taxi with a cigarette. Only Colombians do that."

He asked if I could spare one, so I pulled another cigarette from my pack and passed him my lighter.

I watched the guy sideways as we both smoked. Late forties, maybe. Clean-shaven and pale. Small eyes behind square glasses. Sweatered, with hemmed jeans and brown suede loafers. He smoked vigorously, like a guy who'd been deprived, talking about how this rainstorm was like those of the Amazon, blinding and impossible to navigate. But, he said, rain sounds the same no matter where you are, and he could close his eyes and almost forget this was New York if not for the Midtown smells, the song of car horns, and screeching brakes.

For the first time in a while I wanted to talk but felt my tongue curl into the back of my throat like a sleeping mouse. That very day, my shrink, a guy I'd been seeing three times a week for the past two months and who barely ever said a word even when challenged by my silence, told me I should push myself to talk to a stranger, to make conversation, to *connect*.

When I was down to a nub, I flicked it to the street and lit up another. The guy had the nerve to ask for a second cigarette too. I thought about telling him he could go in the shop behind us and buy his own pack, but just handed one over. He seemed to sense debt accumulating between us and stared at me as I held the lighter out for him.

"Can I invite you to wait out the rain with me over a coffee?"

I said okay because I didn't feel like going home and had no other place to go. On afternoons like that, during the lull between therapy and the night, I often rode the train to the end of the subway line and back just to eat away a few hours, and because it was a way to be with people without really being with people.

We ducked into a coffee shop a few doors down. The exposure was enough to soak the back of my jacket and top of my head. We found a table along the wall. He went to the counter and ordered us two coffees, both black with no sugar. I remember we sat opposite each other as if we'd been assigned to each other for the afternoon, with duty and resignation. He didn't seem particularly curious about me, just that he preferred company to being alone, and maybe it was the same for me.

•

His name was Juan, and he was Colombian going several generations back. This much he revealed on that first afternoon. But he'd abandoned Colombia for Europe a decade earlier and now lived in Madrid with his girlfriend of twenty years and their daughter, who was six. He didn't ask much beyond my name, and my instinct was to tell him a fake one—Sara. But by the end of our coffee, when the rain started to lift, he asked for my number and I gave it. He said we could meet for another coffee sometime. Maybe a walk in a park. We were speaking only Spanish together at this point—I don't recall at which point we'd made the shift—his, with a heavy Bogotá monotone. Without my asking, he admitted he'd recently turned fifty, and I responded that I was twenty-five.

"Look at us," he said, "both partial markers of an incomplete century."

It was only a day before he called. I hadn't worked in two months, since a strange June when I was no longer able to sleep, though nobody knew this. I'd spent entire nights sitting on the stoop of my apartment building, watching people come in and out, pass on the street, waiting for dawn when my eyelids would finally surrender. I'd manage only a two-hour nap every twenty-four hours, and then my heart would begin beating at high velocity, vibrating through my gut and in my throat, and I would fall into a corner on the floor, place my head between the crease of two walls, and weep.

I didn't want Juan to know where I lived, so I agreed to meet him at a café on Elizabeth Street and looped around the whole block so he wouldn't know from which direction I'd come. He appeared even older to me in the September sunlight, face laced with tiny wrinkles, the lens of his frames looked even thicker. He asked if I worked or was in school, so, rather than admit I spent days hiding in my apartment, only venturing out to sell my best clothes at consignment shops as my only income, I took the opportunity to lie again, something I used to feel very guilty about, and invented a whole other life, said I was completing a PhD in anthropology—ridiculous since the only anthropology class I'd ever taken, I'd dropped mid-semester. He asked what I was specializing in and I said the indigenous peoples of the southern Americas, specifically the Sikuani tribe in Colombia because I'd just read an article about how dozens of them had been massacred by paramilitaries for control of their ancestral lands.

I impressed myself with my ability to lie on the fly. It was easier than being honest.

He told me he'd been a lawyer in Colombia, and in Madrid worked as some kind of legal consultant, but he'd given that up last year to pursue his dream of writing a novel that he described as a time-travel supernatural saga about a twenty-first-century Colombian man who travels to ancient Europe and discovers the secrets of destiny, or something like that.

We talked about movies, then books, then about the city: museums and parks and specific streets we each liked to walk. He said he liked to explore neighborhoods at night, and I said I did too.

Then he let slip: "I'm not really supposed to be in this country right now."

"What do you mean?"

"Well, my girlfriend thinks I'm in London. My family thinks I'm in Paris. But I'm here. In this café. With you."

"What are you supposed to be doing in London?"

"Research for my book. That's what I told her. But I was really planning on spending the month in Paris. I have another girlfriend there, you see, and she's been pressuring me to spend more time with her. But when I went to the airport, I canceled my ticket and instead bought one for New York. Nobody knows I'm here."

"Your family knows about the second girlfriend?"

"Yes. They know I've been planning on leaving my girlfriend in Madrid for a long time. If not for our daughter, I would have left years ago."

"I can't imagine spending twenty years with someone, then leaving that person."

"You're young. You will live through many things you never could have imagined."

"I guess you're off the hook because you never took vows."

"A child is a kind of vow. That's why I've come here. To think."

"Maybe you should see a therapist."

"I don't believe in that shit. I've spent years in therapy, and it was useless. My sister is a psychologist, and people pay her a fortune even though she's a lunatic whose own life is a disaster. It's a crime, the industry of therapy. We are all fucked no matter what and when you finally understand that—poof!—you're cured."

When we left each other that afternoon, he kissed me on the cheek in that casual way of every other Colombian on earth, but it felt different, suspended, and I was suddenly aware of his prickly stubble on my cheek, otherwise invisible in daylight.

•

The next day he called to invite me for dinner. He said he would cook. He was staying at the apartment of a friend near the newsstand where we met. I had an appointment with the shrink and would be in the neighborhood anyway, so I agreed but didn't tell him that detail. During my session, I talked about meeting this new stranger.

"You might even call us friends at this point," I said.

The shrink asked if I was experiencing feelings of attraction toward Juan. I said no. Besides, he was old and already had two girlfriends, and I found men who couldn't make up their minds kind of pathetic.

He was staying in one of those cramped old Hell's Kitchen buildings with fire escapes down the front and back where you can hear everything happening in every apartment from the hall. Kids squealing, televisions buzzing. A man yelling that something wasn't his fault.

Normally, if going out with a stranger or to a guy's house for the first time, my friend Thea and I would tell each other exactly where we were headed with names and addresses, but today I hadn't told her or anyone anything. My shrink got me to admit a few weeks earlier that I was harboring anger toward Thea because she'd been the only person I told what happened, and her response was that he was my boyfriend, he was *allowed* to do with me what he wanted, and I was the girlfriend, so I had to take it.

"It's not uncommon and it doesn't mean he's a bad person," she'd said. "All women go through it. You need to forget it and move on."

I knocked on the door marked 302, and Juan swung it open, an apron folded around his waist. He led me into the apartment, a rectangular studio with a queen-size bed pushed into the corner, a small living area along the long wall, and most other walls lined with bookshelves, framed posters of old European films, photographs and postcards thumbtacked to vacant patches of Sheetrock.

I sat on an armchair while Juan dipped into the tiny kitchen and returned with a bottle of wine, which he poured into a pair of glasses already set on the coffee table. He toasted to meeting new friends, to the unknown, and we both sipped, though I kept my lips pressed tight so no wine would slip into my mouth.

Juan cooked pasta. We ate from plates set on our laps. He said he loved cooking, but their chef in Madrid never let him, and the girl-friend in Paris always wanted to go to restaurants. He learned to cook the few years he'd lived on his own in Bogotá. In his childhood home, men weren't allowed in the kitchen.

"Why did you leave Colombia?"

"The same reason everyone leaves. Colombia is a rabid dog."

"Do you miss it?"

"Sometimes."

"Why don't you go back?"

He reached for a pack of cigarettes on the coffee table. This time he'd bought his own and offered me one, which I accepted.

He took a long drag.

"I can't go back."

"Why not?"

"Either they'll kill me or I'll kill myself."

I couldn't tell if he was being vague to provoke intrigue or if I was crossing a line of discretion. So I pulled back, my gaze bouncing around the room from books to photographs and the bed made with boarding school tucks and folds.

"Whose apartment is this?" I asked.

"A journalist friend. He's not really a friend, more of an acquaintance. I hate when people use the word *friend* so liberally. He's Dutch. I met him through another acquaintance. We once had pleasant conversation about the Basque resistance, and he offered me his apartment in New York, and I offered him a room in our place in Madrid."

"I was in Madrid once," I said, "but I had a stomach virus and stayed in the hotel room throwing up for four days, and by then it was already time to leave so I saw nothing."

"A reason to return."

"Most cities make me ill, New York included."

"When I returned to Bogotá after several months in the country-side, I developed a terrible case of asthma."

"You became allergic to your hometown."

"So it would appear."

He stood up abruptly and asked if I wanted coffee. I told him I never drink it at night.

"I'm sorry I didn't think to get us dessert."

"It's fine. I should go anyway."

In truth, I had nobody waiting for me anywhere, only a sense that I should keep things in motion, not linger anywhere too long, so I'd leave Juan's place and migrate along city streets, probably walking the fifty blocks home rather than taking the subway or a cab. By the time I got to my building it might be midnight. The nights were still warm enough that I could sit out on the stoop with a light jacket and not feel too cold. Sometimes I brought a book outside with me though I didn't have the concentration to read. Sometimes I tried to write in my journal, but my hand would go limp after writing only a sentence or two.

Juan walked me downstairs to the street. I thanked him for the meal.

"I hope it wasn't too terrible," he said.

I started to feel crowded by his body so close to mine in the door-way, so I walked away without that kiss on the cheek that had become our hello and goodbye custom since yesterday. I didn't think much of it but seconds later, as I crossed the street, he was at my side.

"Sara. Did I do something wrong?"

"No. Why?"

"You just seem, I don't know."

"You don't know because you don't know me," I said.

We were on the corner now, standing by a garbage can as pedes-trians passed close.

"I want you to know something. I'm not sure why I want you to know it. I left Colombia because I was kidnapped. They held me for five months. When they released me, I left the country within a week. I will never go back. Maybe this makes me a traitor, a man with no loyalties, no character."

"I'm sorry that happened to you."

"It happens to many, and usually much worse. Some they take to the jungle for years, so long their own families forget about them. And when they're freed, they don't think to leave their country. I'm lucky in comparison, yet I ran away."

"Survival requires different things of different people." I don't know where in me this came from. It was something I hadn't even begun to understand for myself.

"Can we spend some more time together? I feel comfortable with you. I can't explain it."

I nodded. I felt the same but wasn't yet ready to say so too.

•

I'd known other people who were kidnapped. It's not only a Colombian thing like newspapers and movies want you to think. Guerillas and paramilitaries didn't invent or even perfect the art of secuestro. Governments have always done it much better.

Back in my hometown, a Jersey suburb where everyone had eyes on each other, a girl from my high school was kidnapped by the young couple she babysat for when they went on the run on account of credit card fraud. The girl's parents hired a detective who tracked her down in Jacksonville three months later. She was hooked on pills and heroin. Our mothers were friendly, so I overheard whispers that even after rehab the girl was never the same, and my father never let me babysit for gringo families after that.

In college, the mother of a girl from my Modern Art class disappeared while walking the family dog on First Avenue. The professor canceled class one day so that we could all help post signs with the mother's picture around Central Park and the Upper East Side. Months passed with no clues, and people muttered the husband should be a suspect though he was never charged. With the spring thaw, a jogger spotted the mother's body on the banks of the East River, fully clothed, still wearing her wedding ring and her gold watch. Police never figured out who did it. The dog was never found.

I heard a television shrink once say the easiest people to hurt are those who've never been hurt before. They're the ones who never see it coming, and afterward, it takes a long time for them to understand what's been done to them.

"He loves you," Thea said. "You have to forgive and let go."

I wondered why it had become my burden.

He once told me that, as a kid, when his father was upset with him or one of his brothers, he would take them alone to a toolshed at the far end of the house property. He'd have the boy sit on a folding chair, tie his arms with a rope behind him, blindfold him, and whip him with a power cord, going much harder if the boy cried. This would last an hour. Maybe two. When it was over, the father would untie the son, fall to his knees, and cry over the child's lap, saying it hurt him to have to do this to his own flesh and blood, but he'd had no choice.

I'd come home from a party with Thea, barely able to hold my head up or walk straight; a reaction from a couple of cocktails mixed with antibiotics for strep throat I'd finished the day before. He was waiting outside my building when we pulled up in a cab. He must have been there for hours. Thea handed me off.

"You take care of her," she said.

He helped me up to my apartment and into bed. I remember, in that moment, feeling grateful for him.

•

Juan said he'd never smoked his entire life until he was taken, when the guards started giving him cigarettes to stave off his hunger. They came for him while he was in a taxi, which is why he still felt a reflexive terror whenever he got into a yellow cab. At a red light on a quiet road on the way to visit his parents in Los Rosales, a car parked close behind them and before he blinked, a machine gun had already poured into the taxi driver's skull and another man was pulling Juan out the door and shoving him into the other car. Juan reached for his wallet, told them to take all his money, but they laughed, said they didn't want his money, they wanted his life.

They were kids, he says. Boys who'd been born and bred to die young, who spoke in indecipherable slang and code, whom he'd get to know by their voices since they'd never let themselves be seen without masks. They made him lie on the car floor, slipped a pillowcase over his head with slits for his nose and mouth, and held their boots tight on his back and neck while another drove for what felt like hours, far enough that when he was pulled out of the car, the air was different, fresh and wet like the sabana air at his family's finca in Subachoque.

They put him in a windowless room the size of a pantry, and now, he said, he felt most comfortable in small quarters, like the apartment of the Dutch man and his second girlfriend's tiny chambre de bonne in Paris. There was a bare mattress on the floor on which he spent most of his day. There was a lamp in the ceiling and they would often remove the bulb to taunt him or to control his waking and sleep patterns. At night, the guards sometimes led him into another room where there was a window with curtains drawn, and a radio and a TV, and he saw his picture flash across the news as the presenter reported there was still no clue of his whereabouts. On the radio, he heard the voices of both his parents pleading to his captors for his release. The masked boys laughed, lifting the fabric that concealed them only enough to bring a joint to their lips. They were high much of the time, Juan said, but still had rules, like that he had to bow his head and raise his right hand for permission to speak or use the toilet. The first few weeks they beat him regularly. Then they went for stretches in a kind of peace, cohabiting, eating the same crummy mushed rice-and-bean slop for every meal with an occasional sausage, bringing Juan a pillow and a blanket for his mattress. But then they would get a visit from a superior, or they would get drunk, and burst into his cell and beat him into a corner, pull his hair, poke their fingers into his eyeballs, spit in his mouth, or piss on his face.

We were in my apartment when he told me this. I had called him this time. It was late, and I knew another long night was ahead for me. He arrived quickly. I put out a bowl of chips and made tea. We sat on the sofa along the window, cracked it open enough to let out our smoke but not let in too much city dust or noise of fire trucks roaring from one end of Fourteenth Street to the other. He spoke calmly, often pausing. He said the boys told him that in these cases, when someone is held captive alone, it's because that person is going to be killed. Otherwise he would have been placed in a house already holding two or three others, which was easier for them to manage until their release.

"So you're going to kill me," he'd said, and one boy punched him for speaking out of turn, removed the light bulb, and locked him in his room.

I got the feeling Juan was waiting for me to ask why he'd been a target. There must have been a reason they saw him as valuable. But I never thought to ask what kind of ransom had been demanded for his freedom or if it had been paid.

Finally, he said, "My family is, well, a word for it would be *prominent*."

"Like drug dealers?"

He laughed. "More like presidents and senators, on both sides."

I wondered which presidents he was related to. Most of the recent ones weren't anything to brag about.

The day of his release, the boys drove Juan to a parking lot behind some warehouses near the airport, that same pillowcase around his head, and told him to count to one hundred very slowly before taking it off. He was so scared he counted to five hundred, sure they were watching and waiting and this was some kind of test. But when he removed his hood, he saw he was alone and heard the rush of nearby traffic. He walked until he came to a boulevard and asked a shop-keeper to use his phone. He called his mother.

To this day, he said, his girlfriend still threw in his face that Juan hadn't called her first. That was another reason he'd stayed with her this long: guilt.

"So why didn't they kill you?" I asked.

Juan shrugged.

"Either I was worth more than they thought, or not worth enough."

•

I remember it started to rain, so I closed the window, but Juan asked me to leave it open an inch. He said when his captors were holding him for two or three months already, he built up the courage to ask for permission to look out the window in the room where they kept the TV and radio. He could hear the soft drum of rain through the walls, feel humidity in his bones, but he wanted to see the rainfall, he wanted to smell it. The boys agreed to part the curtain for him only this once and let Juan sit on a chair by the open window, his hands tied tightly behind his back and with duct tape covering his mouth so he couldn't scream. This is how Juan understood his prison must be in a populated area even though from the window all he saw was a small field surrounded by a high wall, the rise of the Andes in the distance. And it was on those mountain peaks, that charcoal open sky of equatorial dusk, and on that smell of rain on grass and trees, that Juan meditated for two or three minutes until he was sent back to the hard edges and walls and darkness.

We'd smoked the last of the cigarettes and had been listening to the radio so long the station was repeating songs for the third and fourth time. Even the street had gone quiet. Juan's lids were drooping, he rested his head on an elbow propped along the back of the couch, his body turned to me from his end while I leaned against the opposite armrest.

I stood up, went to my bedroom, and returned with a pillow. I pulled a spare blanket, one I only ever used in winter, from a closet and placed it on the cushion beside him.

"You can sleep here. It's a good couch. People like it."

He gave me a tired smile and nodded as if he'd known this is where we were headed all along. I said good night and went to my room without turning back. I locked the door behind me but stood by the wall that separated us for a while, listening for movement, but there was nothing.

That night, I slept. It didn't happen right away. I lay on my bed, my spine resisting the flatness of the mattress. I pulled the blanket over me, pushed it off, then pulled it back on, over my shoulders and head to block out the white streetlights streaking through the blinds and across the walls and ceiling. My face grew hot, so I pushed the blanket back down around my waist, wondering what I would have done in Juan's place, if held captive, if upon being freed my absence would have made my family and friends love me more.

Sometimes I sat at a table with my parents and brother, surrounded by the circus hum of a crowded restaurant, hating that they could not see into me. They'd ask why I was so serious all the time, why so quiet, tell jokes to provoke me to smile. It wasn't their fault, really, that particular blindness. But I couldn't explain. It would break them to know they'd protected me with their lives and failed.

Juan said his parents had prayed to la Virgen del Socorro to protect him, so when he was released they made him promise to name any future daughter after her to show his gratitude. But during captivity, despite having prayed more than ever before, he'd become a complete atheist. His girlfriend didn't care to keep the promise either. So when their daughter was born they'd called her Azul simply because it was their favorite color, and his mother cried for days because they'd given her granddaughter such a meaningless name.

"It's so easy to break a parent's heart," he said. "I keep a distance from my daughter for that very reason. I'm afraid she'll hurt me the way I've hurt my parents. One day I will regret it, I'm sure, but it's the best I can do for now."

I don't know at which point my thoughts turned to dreams. Only that they led me to the hazy consciousness of morning and I realized I slept more that night with Juan in the next room than I had in months.

•

It was the last of the summerlike days before the thorny autumn turn toward winter. Juan and I were on a bench on the riverside, watching the sunset over New Jersey. The sky, graffitied with purple and fuchsia and smoky blue clouds, reflected off the Hudson. It hadn't rained in days.

For weeks, we'd made a routine of sleeping in the same apartment nearly every night. Mostly at my place, Juan on the sofa, curled on the cushions in his trousers and button-downs, taking off only his shoes but never his socks, and me in my bed, finally inhabiting full hours of rest. A few times, I went to his place for dinner, and he allowed me to sleep in the bed while he leaned back in the armchair. Once I sat up in the early hours of morning and saw him hunched over a pillow on his knees and told him he could get in the bed, too, it was okay with me. But he only shook his head and closed his eyes and somehow went back to sleep.

He told me on one of those nights, that after sleeping in the small room where they held him all those months, he could sleep anywhere. He'd trained himself, he said, because sleep was the only escape. Now he could have an equally satisfying slumber on a train, a plane, or even while standing on a street corner and holding his eyes shut for a nap of a minute or two.

He would be leaving for Madrid the next day via a connection through London so as to keep up the lie when his girlfriend arrived to meet him at the airport. We'd spent twenty nights together, and I'd never once heard him on the phone with either of his girlfriends or even his daughter. I never even heard his cell phone ring.

He invented these ways to disappear, he said, because he'd learned all those years ago how it felt to be forgotten, and in some perverse way, he'd grown to like it.

When it was dark, we started the walk back to my apartment. He held my hand at times, the length of a block or two. I wondered what passersby thought when they looked at us, what was their immediate impression. A man and a young woman twenty-five years apart, though we shared no resemblance, so there was no way we could be father and daughter. And there was still a distance between us, a raw awkwardness that never dissipated despite all our shared nights that would make it obvious to anyone that we could not be lovers.

The farewell was not a farewell, really, because he'd planned to come back to New York in late November, and I had no plans that would take me anywhere else.

"We'll see each other again soon," he said.

We exchanged contact information, and it was only when I wrote out my email address for him that I realized I still hadn't told him my real name.

He wasn't mad when I confessed. Not even surprised.

"I'll still call you Sara, if that's okay with you."

•

In the ten years since, I have often wondered if any of what Juan told me was true. The taxi secuestro. The months of imprisonment. He could have gathered those details from any news report or documentary about real kidnapping victims. There have been so many.

I couldn't even be sure the story of the two girlfriends was true. I'd never seen pictures. But then I'd feel bad about my skepticism. He was a man who claimed to have been forced to give proof of his life through an audio cassette with a machine gun aimed at his head, while reciting headlines from that day's *El Tiempo* and recalling the names of his favorite stuffed animals from childhood so that his parents would believe it was their son.

We never saw each other after that September.

November came, and I didn't hear from him. I sat at my computer some nights, running my fingertips over the keyboard, wondering if I should send him a note but I never did. I could have searched the Internet for archived details of his kidnapping, but neither of us had told the other our last names.

A year later, I left New York. I moved to Miami, where I slept heavily through the night and awoke to the sound of doves outside my window and the aroma of sweet morning dew. Here, it rains often, and I welcome the tropical aguaceros, letting water run over my face, drip off my chin, tasting it on my lips, salty and cool and soothing like bits of ocean. I remembered Juan telling me that when he was released and finally returned to the safety of his parents' home, the first thing he did was to go out to the garden and rub dirt on his face, run his hands over the bark of the trees, crush bunches of leaves in his palms, and smell the air that, while dusty and polluted, was at least not the stale air of that windowless box of a room. He'd lay for hours on his back staring at the open sky, even as allergies and asthma kicked in, and even as police came to interview him over and over about his captors. When it rained, he let himself be soaked, eyes closed, remembering the months he'd had to beg for a shower, when that room he existed in might as well have been a desert. He never felt freer, he told me, but with night came the cold and he had no choice but to go indoors, where unrelenting panic returned, and it was quickly decided he and his girlfriend should leave for Spain, where his parents and the police agreed they would be safer.

A few years ago, while in Madrid for the wedding of a friend, I sat by a fountain in El Retiro one afternoon and was sure I saw Juan walking by, looking older, thinner, grayer. I followed him for several meters but as I approached, I realized it was someone else.

I thought of calling or writing him, though he'd never done so, but convinced myself that if we were to see each other again, neither of us would have anything to say.

After a recent visit, my mother left some Colombian magazines behind for me on the kitchen table. It's there, while thumbing through an old issue of *Semana* that I recognize a face printed in color, enlarged to fill the whole page. The rest of the spread shows shots of a funeral. Women dressed in black, wearing dark glasses, exiting a church with arms linked.

I read that the funeral is for a man named Juan, who died of a pulmonary embolism while vacationing in Marbella. The photos of the mourners are captioned with the names of his parents, his longtime companion, and his daughter, Azul, now sixteen.

The article says that despite having made his home in Spain for the last twenty years, it was the family's wishes that Juan's body be returned to Colombia for burial in the family plot.

It listed his famous relatives, presidents and senators, just as he'd told me, and made reference to the months he spent in captivity followed by a heavily negotiated release.

He was fortunate to survive, the article said, when so many others don't.

What stayed with me most was when Juan told me that even though people called him brave for having endured his imprisonment, he considered himself a coward because he hadn't had the courage to try to escape. Instead, he'd spent months waiting for permission to be free, and the shame of this truth, he said, would never leave him.

CREDITS

"Aida" was published in *The Best American Mystery Stories* (2014) and *Harvard Review.*

"Fausto" was published in *A Public Space.*

"The Book of Saints" was published in *The Sun.*

"Campoamor" was published in *The Best American Short Stories* (2017) and *Chicago Quarterly Review.*

"Guapa" was published in *Chicago Quarterly Review.*

"La Ruta" was published in *Prairie Schooner.*

"Ramiro" was published in *Zyzzyva.*

"The Bones of Cristóbal Colón" was published in *Faultline.*

"Aguacero" was published in *The O. Henry Prize Stories 2019* and *Kenyon Review.*

ACKNOWLEDGMENTS

My infinite gratitude to Ayesha Pande, Lauren Wein, Alexandra Primiani, Meredith Vilarello, Amy Guay, and the extraordinary teams at Pande Literary, Avid Reader Press, and Simon & Schuster; to the journals and editors who first published these stories; to my colleagues and students at the University of Miami Creative Writing Program. To my readers; to my dearest friends; to my writing companions; to my family, far and near; to Richard; to John Henry; to Matías, my shining star; and to my ancestors. To my beloved mother, who departed this life shortly before these stories became a book, and to my father: every word is for you.

ABOUT THE AUTHOR

PATRICIA ENGEL is the author of *Infinite Country*, a *New York Times* bestseller, Reese's Book Club selection, and winner of the New American Voices Award; *The Veins of the Ocean*, winner of the Dayton Literary Peace Prize; *It's Not Love, It's Just Paris*, winner of the International Latino Book Award; and *Vida*, a finalist for the Pen/Hemingway and Young Lions Fiction Awards, *New York Times* Notable Book, and winner of Colombia's national book award, the Premio Biblioteca de Narrativa Colombiana. She is a recipient of fellowships from the Guggenheim Foundation and the National Endowment for the Arts. Her stories appear in *The Best American Short Stories*, *The Best American Mystery Stories*, *The O. Henry Prize Stories*, and elsewhere. Born to Colombian parents, Patricia is an associate professor of creative writing at the University of Miami.